SECOND CHANCE

DI023753

Second Chance

LEFT BEHIND

>THE KIDS<

Jerry B. Jenkins

Tim LaHaye

TYNDALE HOUSE PUBLISHERS, INC.
WHEATON, ILLINOIS

Visit Tyndale's exciting Web site at www.tyndale.com

Discover the latest Left Behind news at www.leftbehind.com

Copyright © 1998 by Jerry B. Jenkins and Tim LaHaye. All rights
reserved.

Cover photo copyright © 1995 by Mark Green. All rights reserved.
Cover photo copyright © 1987 by Robert Flesher. All rights reserved.

Left Behind is a registered trademark of Tyndale House Publishers, Inc.

Published in association with the literary agency of Alive
Communications, Inc., 7680 Goddard Street, Suite 200,
Colorado Springs, CO 80920.

Scripture taken from the New King James Version. Copyright © 1979,
1980, 1982 by Thomas Nelson, Inc. Used by permission. All rights
reserved.

Designed by Brian Eterno
Edited by Rick Blanchette

ISBN 0-8423-2194-2

Printed in the United States of America

05   04   03   02   01
25   24   23   22   21   20   19

To Jim Pearl

CONTENTS

ONE

New Hope

JUDD Thompson Jr. had always sized up situations quickly. It was clear to him that of the four kids who had fled to nearby New Hope Village Church during the greatest crisis the world would ever see, he was the oldest. The redhead, the only girl, had a hard, bitter edge to her. But still, if Judd had to guess, he would have said she was younger than he was.

Ah, what did he care. How could he ever care about anything anymore? The end of the world, at least the world as he knew it, had come. Millions all over the world had disappeared right out of their clothes, leaving everything but flesh and bone behind.

It wasn't that Judd didn't know what had happened. He knew all too well. As he had heard in church and Sunday school and at

1

home his whole life, Jesus Christ had come back to rapture his church, and Judd had been left behind.

He even knew why. It didn't take the earnest visitation pastor of New Hope Village Church, Bruce Barnes, to explain that. Of all things, Pastor Barnes himself had been left behind.

Bruce Barnes had spent the last several minutes telling Judd and the three other shell-shocked kids his own story. He finished by telling them there was still hope. Life would be miserable from now on, of course, and they would be alone except for other new believers, but it was not too late for them to come to Christ.

Bruce had urged them to think about it and not to waste much time. The world had become dangerous overnight. With so many Christians disappearing from important jobs, the result was chaos. No one had any guarantees. Life was fragile. Judd was impressed that Bruce seemed so eager to convince them that their only hope now was to trust Christ.

Judd knew it was the truth. He had to face himself, and he didn't like what he saw. His whole look, the way he carried himself, the me-first attitude, the secret that he had never really become a Christian—all those things sickened him now.

Why had he wanted to appear so old? Why was it so important to him to know where he fit in every crowd? Everything that ever mattered to him now seemed ridiculous. He had been a tough guy, a big shot, the one with all the plans and schemes. He had stolen his dad's credit card and bought phony identification papers that said he was old enough to travel on his own. *Yeah,* Judd thought, *I was a real player.*

But though Judd had come to some hard realizations about himself, he still had a major problem. There was no question Bruce was right. Judd didn't want to live without his family and without Christ. Though he knew he had had every chance and could have been in heaven with his parents and brother and sister right then, everything in him still fought to blame somebody else. But whom could he blame?

His parents had been wonderful examples to him. Even his little brother had recently asked Judd if he still loved Jesus. If he couldn't blame his family and he didn't want to blame himself, that left only God. He knew there was no future in blaming a perfect and holy God, but right then he had to admit that he didn't much care for God's plan.

Whatever happened to the idea that God loved everybody and didn't want anybody to die and go to hell? What kind of a God would leave a sixteen-year-old kid without his family?

Judd knew he wasn't thinking straight. In fact, he had to admit he was being ridiculous. But just then he didn't like God very much. He was mad at God because there was no one else to be mad at.

Besides, Judd was grieving. No, his family had not died. But they might as well have. He was glad for them, he guessed, that they had gotten their reward for believing. But that was of little comfort to him.

Bruce Barnes asked the four kids to introduce themselves and talk about themselves a bit. Judd didn't see the point of that. Bruce began with the youngest boy, the little blond who appeared stocky and athletic.

Judd was reminded of his own little brother, Marc. Marc and Marcie were twins, nine years old. Both had been tremendously athletic. While Judd had lost interest in sports after Little League, Marc and Marcie had seemed interested in every sport imaginable. They had both been dark-haired and younger and smaller than Ryan Daley, but still Judd found it hard to listen to the boy without thinking of them both. Already he missed them more than he could say. Just being around someone even near their age cut like a knife deep into his heart.

Ryan was telling his story at just above a whisper. Judd could tell the boy had spent a lot of time crying that day. No doubt there would be more tears until he could cry no more.

"I don't know what I think about all this stuff you've been saying, Mr. Barnes. If it's true, I don't think either of my parents went to heaven. For sure my mom didn't because she was killed on the road sometime this morning. My dad was listed with the passengers that went down in a plane crash. I don't think he would have been one of those who disappeared. I mean, he was great and I loved him, but he never said anything about being a Christian or even going to church."

Ryan told about waking up to find his mother's note and then hearing from the police about her death. When he stopped and buried his head in his hands, Bruce Barnes leaned forward and put a hand on his shoulder. "So you've never, ever been in church before?"

"Well, not never," Ryan managed, raising his head. "Somebody invited me to one of those Bible school things they have in the summertime at church once—"

"Vacation Bible School?" Bruce said.

"Yeah, that's it. But I was really little then and I don't remember much about it. My friend—his dad's an airline pilot—wanted me to go to church with him here. I never did."

"And who was that?"

"His name was Raymie Steele. He tried to tell me all about this, the way you just did. I thought he was nuts."

"What do you think now, Ryan?"

With that, Ryan buried his face in his hands again and sobbed. Bruce began to ask him something, but Ryan wrenched away and shook his head. Judd thought he knew exactly how Ryan felt.

Bruce turned to Lionel Washington. Judd noticed that the lanky young boy with the smooth face and chocolate complexion had sat expressionless since they had begun. His wide, dark eyes seemed to rarely blink. He merely sat forward, his chin resting on his fist, listening. Judd couldn't tell if he was interested or not, but something had brought him there.

Bruce asked Lionel if he knew any of the others. "No, but my sister Clarice knew Vicki here. They rode the school bus together."

"How do you feel about all this?" Bruce said.

"Oh," Lionel said, "this is nothing new to me. I know exactly what happened. You're right, we all missed it. The real Christians have gone to heaven, and we've all been left behind."

Ryan leaped from his seat and ran out, shouting through his sobs, "It's not fair! It's not fair! This is crazy! Why would God do this?"

Judd, Bruce, Vicki, and Lionel watched him go. "Aren't you going to stop him?" Judd asked Bruce.

Bruce shook his head. "He'll be back. Where else does he have to go?"

Lionel, who seemed to Judd to have been shaken by Ryan's quick exit, finished his own story of having grown up in a Christian family and gone to church all his life, only to never have made a true decision himself to become a follower of Christ. "I don't know how the rest of you feel, but I can't say I'm surprised or that I didn't get exactly what I deserved. I don't know if I believe there's really still a second chance, but if there is, I want it."

"Believe me, there is a second chance," Bruce said, "and I think it's something you'll want to take advantage of right away, don't you?"

"You better believe I already prayed the prayer," Lionel said. "If that's what you mean. I told God I was sorry, begged his forgiveness, and asked him to save me once and for all. You're saying it's not too late?"

"That's what I'm saying. Welcome to the family."

"To tell you the truth, sir," Lionel said, "I'd rather be in heaven with my own family right now."

"You and me both," Bruce said.

Judd was stunned at how much he and Lionel had in common, though they had never even seen each other before. Lionel, like Judd, also had a younger brother and sister. And Judd and Lionel had been raised in the church by Christian families.

Now it was Vicki's turn. "Well," she began with a quavery voice, "I guess I should have known better too."

Judd noticed how young and scared she sounded for someone who said she was fourteen years old. Of course, he felt very young and scared himself just then, but she looked like a tough girl. Whatever edge there had been to her seemed to have been stolen away when her mother, father, and little sister had been raptured. She told her story about growing up in the trailer park, about the weekend beer brawls and dances that had one time, seemingly out of the blue, begun with an evangelist preaching for just a few minutes and resulted in her parents becoming Christians.

"I saw big changes in their lives," Vicki

admitted, "but actually I hated it. I hated church, and I didn't want to have anything to do with religion. They kept telling me it wasn't religion, it was Jesus, but I didn't see the difference."

"Now you do, of course," Bruce said.

"Of course," she said.

"Forgive me for being pushy," Bruce said, "but what are you going to do about it now?"

Vicki looked down and busied herself tracing a pattern on the floor with the toe of her shoe. "Actually, even though I know you're right, I just don't want to make a decision like this while I'm still in shock."

Bruce seemed to be trying gently to push her into seeing that, despite the trauma she had just been through, she really shouldn't take more time. "You know the truth. That makes it your responsibility to act upon it."

"I know," she whispered. But she would not return his gaze. Her body seemed rigid. To Judd it seemed as if she was through listening or talking about it. He was surprised when she looked up and appeared to be listening when it was his turn to tell his story.

Judd kept his account short. He merely mentioned that he too had been raised in a Christian home and knew exactly what had happened. He told of his plan to run away from home and be his own person, and how it had all come crashing down on him when the Rapture occurred while he was on a plane over the Atlantic on the way to London.

"I have to say, though, Pastor Barnes, I feel like Vicki here. I know what I'm *supposed* to do, what I *should* do, and what I'm sure I *will* do. But I just feel too much pressure. I can hardly get my mind around the fact that I'll never see my family again."

Bruce stood and moved near to Judd. "Don't you kids see? That's my point! If I'm right and a seven-year period of tribulation begins soon, it's unlikely any of us will live through it. We had better be prepared to see God, or we'll wind up without him for all of eternity."

Judd knew Bruce was right, but he caught Vicki's glance and knew the two of them were still determined not to be pushed. He only hoped that it wasn't simply a pride thing. He was pretty sure it wasn't. He was way past pride now.

"I'm sorry, Pastor Barnes, but I just need more time to deal with all of this," Judd said.

"Me too," Vicki said.

"Don't be waiting too long now," Lionel said. "I waited way too long as it is."

"I couldn't have said that better myself," Bruce said.

TWO

Vicki's Journey

IF there was one thing Vicki Byrne was sure of when she left New Hope Village Church that day, it was what she was feeling. No way around it, she decided. She felt guilty.

She stopped at the door and looked back to see Bruce Barnes sitting wearily, hands atop his head, fingers entwined. He was almost imperceptibly shaking his head.

"I'm going to go look for that little kid," Lionel said, excusing himself as he slipped past her and out of the church.

"We'll be back, I'm sure," Judd Thompson was telling Bruce. Vicki was certain of that too, and she felt bad because she understood how much Bruce Barnes cared and how urgent he felt it was that they make their decisions for Christ now.

Vicki started toward home, though it was

the last place she wanted to go. That empty trailer would only remind her how truly alone she was. She hesitated on the sidewalk, noticing the small bicycle someone had left out front. She assumed it was Ryan's. There was nowhere else to go, nothing else to do. She headed on foot for the trailer park.

Judd Thompson called to her from the door of the church. "So, what are you going to do?" he said.

"Same as you," she said. "Think it over. Do the right thing. We both know what that means. I just don't want to do it when I'm so exhausted and keyed up at the same time."

"I know what you mean," Judd said. "But I meant what are you going to do right now?"

"Just go home I guess," she said.

"You want to go somewhere with me?"

"Like where?"

"I've got to go get my father's car. I left it at O'Hare."

Vicki shrugged. "Why not? How are we getting there? We gonna ride double on Ryan's bike?"

"That's my little brother's bike. I'm going to see if Bruce will let me leave that here. I was thinking of taking a cab."

"You must have a lot more money than I do," Vicki said.

"That's one thing I'm not short of," Judd

said. "But I'd trade it all to be in heaven right now."

"I know," Vicki said. "This is awful."

A few minutes later, Marc Thompson's bike was stored just inside the front door of the church and Judd was on the phone to a cab company. It took forever to get a connection and then for someone to answer. He was told there would be a premium on the fare. "What does that mean?" he asked.

"That it's going to cost you triple the normal amount. And we don't recommend trying to get into O'Hare. It's still a mess."

"I need to get my car out of there," Judd said.

"That parking garage is a disaster. A bunch of people disappeared while driving out of there, and their crashed cars left a gridlock that's going to take days to untangle."

"I still have to try," Judd said. "I want to make sure it's OK and get it before someone steals it."

"Suit yourself. Somebody should be there for you within the hour."

Vicki and Judd sat on the curb, waiting. She didn't recall having seen this boy before. Despite his scruffy look, it was clear to her Judd was a rich kid. Their paths would not have crossed for long, had they ever met. Vicki felt an unexplained need to keep some sort of conversation going. Though she hated the idea of facing that trailer, what she really wanted was to get home to her own bed and bury her face in the pillow and cry over all that she had lost. What a waste her life had been, she decided.

Still, she was grateful for something to do, somewhere to go, someone to be with. She asked Judd to tell her more about his family. He cried as he told her, and that made her cry too. "We're both going to have to do the right thing here soon, aren't we?" she said.

"I know," Judd said.

The cab arrived nearly two hours later. "Sorry it took me so long," the cabby said. He was a burly man in a sleeveless T-shirt. He looked as if he could use some sleep. "It's hard for us to get to our call-ins because we're not allowed to pass by anyone who's trying to flag us down on the way."

"And a lot of people are doing that?" Vicki said.

"I had three other rides before I got here," the cabby said. "And I even told another guy to wait for another cab. He wanted to pay me to take him all the way to Wisconsin."

"Wow!"

"You're telling me! I don't think he could have afforded it anyway, but I don't have to take somebody that far when I've got a

call-in. You kids aren't really going to
O'Hare, are you? You know there's nothing
flying out of there—"

"I'm just going to try to get my car out of
there," Judd said.

"That's gonna be no picnic either, son,"
the cabby said.

"I know. But I have to try. I've got nothing
else to do."

Vicki was amazed to see so many fires as
the cab snaked its way through the remains
of car wrecks, traffic gridlocks, even fights. It
was clear there would never be enough local
police to go around. *So this is what it's like at
the end of the world,* she thought.

Where were all these people going? All
Vicki had noticed near the church were sirens
in the distance and the glow of distant fires
on the horizon. Now she could see that those
fires were not so distant. "Why is everything
burning?" she asked.

"You don't know?" the cabby said.
"Nobody knows yet how many people disappeared late last night, but any of them who
had anything on the stove just left it there.
You leave something on the stove overnight,
eventually the food burns up, the water turns
to steam, the pan gets hotter than blazes, and
before you know it your kitchen's on fire.

With nobody there to fight it or report it, boom, there goes your house."

Vicki saw looks of jealousy on the faces of people waving at the cab from street corners, disappointed to see that it was already hired. What a mess. Were all these people just trying to find somewhere, anywhere, that wasn't turning to rubble?

As the night grew dark and the cab slowly picked its way through side streets and back roads toward Interstate 294, Vicki noticed that Judd had seemed to lose interest in talking. He sat with his chin resting in his hands. He had turned away from her and appeared to stare out the window as they slowly rode along. When would it sink in? she wondered. When would she feel her own fatigue and exhaustion and finally be able to sleep? And how would all this feel when she finally woke up and realized it was not a dream, not a nightmare, but reality? How do you go from being part of a family to becoming an orphan overnight? She sighed. She hadn't even liked being in her family. She didn't like it when her parents were loud drunks, and she liked it even less when they became Christians.

Now she realized, of course, that for at least the last two years—since her parents had become believers—she herself had been the problem. She had somehow realized that her life would not be her own if she became a Christian like her parents. They had told her and told her that she didn't need to clean up her life before she came to Christ. "Jesus accepts you just the way you are," her mother had told her. "He'll start showing you what needs to be changed and will help you change."

The problem was, Vicki knew her mother was right. She simply didn't want to change, whether she herself was making the changes or God was. She had liked her life just the way it was because it was just that—her life. Why had it taken this, something so huge, so cosmic, so disastrous to show her how foolish she had been? She had been such a rebel, so mean to her parents and even to her sweet little sister, Jeanni.

And what was with this dolt sitting next to her? Judd Thompson seemed like a nice enough guy, having made the same huge life-and-death mistakes she had made. But had he even once asked her about herself or her family? Sure, she had told her story in the little meeting at New Hope, just like he had. But how was it that she knew to ask for more details, even if just to be polite, and he didn't? Wasn't that just like a rich kid to not care about anybody else? She had a bad feeling that she wasn't going to like this guy very much, despite what they were going through together. Well, she concluded, at least he had asked her to go with him on his errand. That was better than being alone just now.

Of course, she decided, that was the real reason he had invited her anyway. He didn't want to be alone any more than she did. Vicki was finally doing a little something for somebody other than herself. She could serve that purpose. She could keep this poor rich kid from being alone during the worst night of his life.

The tollway to O'Hare was stop-and-go when it was moving at all. Vicki simply didn't understand where all these people were going. But then, she and Judd were going somewhere, so why couldn't everyone else?

The cabby had fallen silent long ago. He kept taking huge swigs from a mug of coffee and opened his window so the cool night air filled the car. Vicki shivered and wished he would shut it, but didn't say anything. The way he looked, he had probably been driving for twenty-four hours. She was not about to discourage anything that would keep him awake.

Within a couple of miles of the airport, the traffic stopped dead. With Judd seemingly still more interested in staring out the window than talking to her and the cab driver appearing to concentrate on simply staying awake, Vicki was alone with her thoughts. It was, she knew, time to talk to God. It would be the first time she had done that in as long as she could remember.

As Vicki rested her face in her hands, she felt movement next to her. She peeked at Judd, who was still turned away from her. His shoulders heaved, and she knew he was sobbing, though he was somehow able to muffle the sounds.

Vicki was suddenly overcome with an emotion she hadn't felt in years. She felt desperately, overwhelmingly sorry for this boy. Maybe he was a rich kid, maybe he was insensitive, maybe he was so selfish he couldn't even be polite. But he was suffering the way she was suffering. She knew exactly how he felt.

Almost without thinking, Vicki put her hand gently on his shoulder. Judd lowered his head to his hands and sobbed aloud. Vicki saw the cab driver's sympathetic glance through the rearview mirror. Judd whispered hoarsely, "I was so stupid. So stupid." Judd moved slightly, and Vicki worried that he might be embarrassed. She pulled her hand away and retreated to her own thoughts.

Fighting a sob in her own throat, she

prayed silently. "God," she said, "I don't even know how to talk to you, let alone what to say. Bruce Barnes said you loved us and cared about us and didn't want to leave us behind. I hope that's true because I want to believe in you. I'm sorry for having been such a bad person, and I'm sorry that it took something like this to make me come to you. I wish I could say I would have done this eventually anyway, but I can't. I had enough chances, but I didn't want to give you my life. If you can forgive me for that and still accept me, you can have whatever is left of my life. For a long time I hoped you weren't real and that I wouldn't have to answer to you someday, but I always knew down deep you were there. And if nothing else convinced me, this mess sure has. I know it can't be as good to believe now when I have no choice, but if you'll accept me, I will live for you for as long as you let me stay alive."

Vicki and Judd sat in silence for almost another two hours while the cab slowly inched its way toward the international airport. Suddenly the cabby pulled off the road and sat on the shoulder, shifting into park. He turned to Judd. "I'm sorry, son, but you can see if I take that exit ramp to O'Hare right there, we might not get out of there for days. You're still a couple of miles from the parking garage, but I think this is as close as I can get you."

Vicki could see he was right. Nothing was moving on that ramp. Judd looked at her, and they both shrugged. Judd paid the driver and thanked him.

Suddenly Vicki found herself alone with a strange boy on a chilly night, on foot in a world that had come apart at the seams.

It was while walking with Judd that fatigue overcame Vicki. She didn't want to say so, but she wondered with each step if she could take another. This had been one long, grueling, horrifying day. Now, she thought, maybe she could finally rest in her own bed. The memories and her loss would still haunt her, but she believed God would allow her to sleep. She knew she didn't deserve to have him in her life, but she could do nothing less now than to trust him and believe in him and depend upon him.

Finally, walking in the grass next to the shoulder of the road, which was filled with cars barely moving, Judd broke his long silence. "Vicki, I've been thinking and praying."

"Me too," she said.

"Really?"

She nodded.

"That's good," he said, "because I don't

think we're smart to put off our decision any longer. Who knows what might happen?"

"So you already became a Christian?" she asked.

He nodded. "I just figured it was really dumb to wait any longer. Not that I'm saying you're dumb, you know."

"I did the same thing a little while ago, Judd. If what Bruce said is true, then I guess that puts us in the same family. We're brother and sister now."

Judd nodded again. "I guess we are," he said. "I could use a sister."

"I could use a brother."

"Yeah, didn't you say your big brother was living in Michigan and you thought he was raptured too?"

"I thought you'd never ask."

THREE

Lionel's Shock

LIONEL Washington had sprinted down the street away from New Hope Village Church, looking both ways for any sign of Ryan Daley. He knew the little guy had gotten quite a head start on him and only hoped that Ryan was not still running. If he was, Lionel would never catch him.

Lionel was a fast runner, but this was ridiculous. He huffed and puffed and sucked air, running in the general direction of his own house. He hoped Ryan's home was somewhere on the way. Maybe the kid had to stop and catch his breath himself.

Lionel slowed to a walk and put his hands on his hips, allowing his chest to expand and his lungs to drink in more air.

He squinted at a small form huddled under a street lamp two blocks ahead. It could have been anybody, of course, as people just like him—people who had lost loved ones and were scared to death and wondering what was going on—wandered about hoping to see someone they knew.

When Lionel was within a block of the streetlight, the form rose and began to walk. It was Ryan Daley. This time, fortunately, he was not running. At least not until he turned and looked behind him. When he saw Lionel, he began to jog.

"Hey! Hey, kid!" Lionel called. For the moment, he had forgotten the boy's name. "Wait up!"

At first Ryan seemed to speed up, but then it appeared he had resigned himself to the fact that there was nowhere to go anyway. He stepped off the sidewalk into the grass and thrust his hands deep in his pockets, his chin tucked to his chest. Lionel figured he had been crying. Maybe he still was. He sure didn't have to be ashamed of that, Lionel thought.

Lionel hurried to the boy and stood next to him, matching his posture, pushing his hands into his pockets and looking down. "What are you gonna do?" Lionel said. In his peripheral vision, Lionel saw Ryan shrug. "Ryan, isn't it?" Lionel said. "That's your name, right?" Lionel looked up in time to see

Ryan nod slightly. "Ryan, I know how you feel. This is terrible, and we all hate it."

"How could you know how I feel?" Ryan blurted. "Your family's in heaven. For all I know, my parents aren't just dead, they're in hell."

Lionel didn't know what to say. He believed that was true. Nothing he said could make that any better. "The important thing now is," he finally managed, "what are *you* gonna do?"

Ryan sat in the grass in the darkness and put his face between his knees. Though his voice was muffled, Lionel could make out what he was saying. "I have no idea what I'm gonna do. I'm not going to be able to stand being in that house all by myself, I know that. I thought maybe I'd just gather up a bunch of stuff and pitch my tent in the back-yard. I guess I can stand going in there for food and the bathroom, but I wouldn't want to live in there. And I sure wouldn't want to sleep in there."

"Me either," Lionel said. "My house has my family's clothes all over the place, right where they left them when they disappeared."

"I wish mine did," Ryan said. "Then I wouldn't have to believe all this stuff about everybody who disappeared going to heaven."

Lionel nodded, but said nothing.

"I don't s'pose you'd want to help me get my tent set up?"

"Sure I would," Lionel said. "I've got nothing else to do."

"It's just a couple of blocks from here," Ryan said. "Thanks, Lyle."

"It's Lionel."

"Sorry. Like the train?"

"Uh-huh."

A few minutes later Lionel and Ryan were digging around in the garage at Ryan's house. Lionel saw Ryan occasionally looking at the door that led into the kitchen. "You want something in there?" Lionel said. "I'll get it for you."

"I *am* getting a little hungry," Ryan said. "It's just that I don't want to go in there yet."

"I'll get you whatever you want," Lionel said. "You want me to just find whatever I can in the refrigerator and the cupboards?"

The Daleys' kitchen was similar to Lionel's own. He could hear Ryan dragging stuff from the garage to the backyard, and he hoped the boy would invite him to stay. Lionel would have to go home and get some of his stuff, but he didn't want to be in his house any more than Ryan wanted to be in this one.

Lionel found a bunch of snacks and soft drinks and went directly into the backyard from the kitchen. He wondered if Ryan would be too shy to invite him. "You want some company tonight?" Lionel offered.

"You'd stay with me?"

"Sure! I don't want to be alone tonight any more than you do."

Once the tent was set up—snacks, flashlights and all—the boys headed toward Lionel's house, just over a mile away. Ryan wasn't saying much. Lionel had never been a big talker either, but when he wasn't talking he felt like crying, and he assumed Ryan felt the same. "I guess we don't have to worry about going to school tomorrow," Lionel said.

"Yeah. I heard on the news that enough students and teachers and parents disappeared that it might be a long time before school opens again."

Lionel snorted. "So we can be thankful for a little good news in all this mess." That wasn't really funny, of course. This was a nightmare from which neither of them would awaken.

Lionel figured Ryan was just as tired as he was by the time they reached Lionel's house. "You want to come in for a minute while I get my stuff?"

"It beats being outside alone, I guess."

The first thing Lionel noticed in the kitchen was that the answering machine was emitting a steady tone that indicated the tape was completely full of messages. Ryan followed him upstairs as Lionel ignored his parents' and his sisters' bedrooms and grabbed a backpack that he stuffed with clothes. On the way down he turned toward the kitchen to listen to the messages, noticing that Ryan was no longer behind him. Lionel turned to see Ryan staring at Lionel's father's nightclothes draped over the chair in the living room. "C'mon, man," Lionel said. "That gives me the creeps just as much as it does you."

White people were nothing new to Lionel, of course, and he wasn't surprised that a blond boy was paler than most. But he had never seen a face as ghostlike as Ryan's when he turned away from those empty clothes in the living room. Ryan appeared to be gasping for breath. Lionel wanted to get Ryan's mind off what he had just seen. "Let me listen to these messages," he said, "and then we'll go."

Lionel played the answering machine tape for several minutes before getting past the messages he had already heard that morning. He was stunned then to hear that the entire rest of the tape was just one long, rambling message from none other than his uncle André.

As soon as Lionel began listening to it, he wished he hadn't turned it on. He wished even more that Ryan was not there to hear it. It was clear Uncle André was either drunk or high or both. His grief and his horror were obvious. "Lionel, man," he said, "I done you wrong. I led you down the wrong path, boy. I just called to tell you I'm sorry and to say good-bye. I never meant to do wrong by you. I hope you'll find it in yourself to forgive me someday. I should have been there for you, and I should stay here and be here for you now, but I just can't. I can't live with myself."

Lionel had never heard anything like that before, but it sure sounded like André was planning to kill himself. Lionel listened with urgency, hoping and praying he would hear some clue about where André was calling from.

A couple of times Lionel thought he heard voices in the background and wondered if André's enemies—the ones he owed money to—had put him up to this. Maybe they wanted it to sound like he was planning suicide when actually they were going to kill him. Lionel didn't want his imagination to run away with itself. This was bad enough. André was serious. Dead serious.

Lionel sneaked a glance at Ryan, who still appeared ashen and seemed to be barely breathing. Lionel turned the machine off. "Maybe you don't want to hear this," he said.

"No, it's all right. You'd better find out

where he's calling from or we'll never be able to help him."

"I'm not going to drag you into this. This guy is my uncle, and I'll need to handle it myself."

"Don't keep me out of this, Lionel!" Ryan said. "I got to keep myself busy or I'll be thinking about the same thing your uncle is thinking about."

"Let's hope he's still just thinking about it."

Lionel turned the machine on again and could hear what sounded like a bottle being poured into a glass. Also, if he had to guess, he would have assumed André was downing some pills. André's voice became slower and more slurred, and he cried more as he spoke. "Lionel, don't make the same mistakes I made. I was wrong, totally wrong. I heard all my life that God loved me and that Jesus died for me and that I was a sinner. I knew it. I believed it. I just never bought into it for myself. I told you a lot of it was fairy tales, and I hoped I was right. But I was wrong. I was wrong."

Lionel didn't think he had any more tears to shed, but he could feel them welling up again. André sounded so lost, so empty. Lionel thought about whom he could call, where he could possibly find André. He wondered if anyone left behind at the church might have any idea where André was. He flipped off the machine and dialed the church. The line was busy. He tried time and again, but always it was busy. He asked Ryan to take over and keep dialing. Meanwhile, he listened to the rest of the tape, which went on for more than twenty minutes. In it, his uncle André simply repeated how sorry he was, how sick he was of himself, how much he hated his life, and what a waste it had been. In the end, he resorted to simply apologizing over and over and saying good-bye. He was still talking, mumbling, rambling, when the tape ran out.

Ryan said, "It's ringing!"

Lionel grabbed the phone. When the machine at the church picked up, however, it merely signaled a long tone as well. The tape was full, and no one was there to answer either.

"I've got to get to André's place," Lionel said.

"Where's that?" Ryan said.

"In Chicago."

"How are you going to get there?"

"On my bike, I guess," Lionel said. "You want to go with me?"

"Sure. But I've never ridden a bike to Chicago."

"You can use my sister's bike," Lionel said.

"No, I've got my own. Just give me a ride back to my house and I'll get mine."

Half an hour later, Lionel and Ryan were pedaling quickly out of Mount Prospect, heading toward Chicago. Lionel hoped he would recognize the same landmarks he did while riding in the car. It seemed to take so long to get to each one while riding bikes. He soon realized he was going too fast to keep up his endurance. "Let's slow down," he hollered. "Let's save our strength. It's going to be a long trip."

The boys reached André's neighborhood around eleven o'clock. Lionel had never been out that late alone before, and he was intrigued that no one seemed to mind. He couldn't imagine riding his bike through cordoned-off expressways and side streets on his way to the inner city of Chicago without being stopped by the police. It simply seemed too strange that two young boys would be out on their bikes in Chicago at this time of the night.

Had it not been for his grief and his fear and his anxiety over Uncle André, Lionel might have enjoyed an adventure like this. But just then he couldn't imagine ever enjoying anything again. He sure hoped Bruce Barnes was right and that he was still eligible to become a Christian, even at this late date. It was awful that he had missed the truth the first time around, especially when he knew better. He sure didn't want to live through a period like this and lose out on heaven altogether.

"How do your legs feel?" Lionel asked Ryan. "Tight and heavy?"

"Yeah," Ryan said. "I can't imagine riding all the way back to Mount Prospect tonight."

"But we have to," Lionel said. "The only people I would want to stay with down here are all gone. I wouldn't feel safe with the ones who are left."

When Lionel and Ryan came within sight of the tacky little hotel where André rented a room, a couple of policemen were getting back into their cruiser. The one getting in the passenger side noticed the boys. "No time to even deal with you two tonight," he said. "Why don't you just run along home?"

"I'm looking for someone," Lionel said.

"Who isn't?" the cop said.

"My uncle lives in this building," Lionel said. He gave the officer André's full name.

The cops glanced at each other with what Lionel sensed was a knowing look. "Should I tell him?" the one cop said to the other.

The driver shrugged. "Why not?"

"Son, your uncle is the reason we were called off traffic duty, where we've been all day. He was found in his apartment a couple of hours ago. His body was just loaded onto an ambulance and taken to one of the morgues set up at a high school about seven blocks down the street here."

"A morgue?" Lionel said, his voice tight.

"Yeah. Sorry."

"How did he die?"

"I'm not at liberty to tell you that, son. You can take it up with the people at the morgue. I'm real sorry, but we've gotta go. You boys should be getting back home now. You've got somebody to go to?"

"We'll be all right," Lionel said. But he wasn't all right, and he knew Ryan wasn't either.

Lionel realized that he and Ryan finally had something in common. Now they both had people they loved who were dead and gone, and not to heaven.

Lionel thought he should identify his uncle's body, but he didn't want to see André that way. He didn't really want to know how André killed himself either, if that was really the way he died. What difference did it make whether he had killed himself or was murdered? He was gone. There was no more hope for him. And Lionel had one more reason to grieve.

Lionel and Ryan rode back to Ryan's house in silence. The trip home took even longer than the trip to Chicago. Ryan seemed as

starved as Lionel felt, and they stuffed crack-
ers in their mouths and washed them down
with soft drinks before stretching out in the
tent. It was well after midnight by now, and
Lionel heard Ryan whimpering in the dark.
He was crying himself to sleep.

And Lionel did the same.

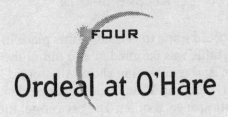

FOUR

Ordeal at O'Hare

Judd and Vicki reached the entrance road to O'Hare, just past Mannheim Road, late in the evening, about the time Lionel and Ryan were heading back to Mount Prospect from Chicago.

Judd had never seen anything like this in his life. He and Vicki found themselves wandering, along with hundreds, maybe thousands of others, who were coming to or going from the giant airport for a variety of reasons. Many, it was clear, had come to O'Hare hoping to find a friend or loved one alive. The people coming the other way, those exiting the airport, had either been unable to get their cars out of the parking garage or unable to find a taxi or limo to get them home.

It was hard for Judd to imagine how any-

one could hope to get out of this place in a
car. Traffic was jammed in and out of the
place, and tempers ran short. All around
them, Judd and Vicki could hear people
shouting at each other. The occasional limo
or cab would break from the pack and race
along the grassy median and up onto Mannheim Road or another artery.

As they got closer and closer to the massive
parking garage, Judd struck up conversations
with others who were on missions similar to
his. "Doesn't look like we're gonna be getting
our cars out of here tonight," a middle-aged
man groused to Judd.

"Nope," Judd said. "But I have to try anyway."

"I see lots of activity up there, cranes, tow
trucks, cops. I don't know what they're
doing."

"I don't either," Judd said. "I parked at the
end of one row, so maybe I'll get lucky."

"Don't count on it."

At the parking garage, cops with bullhorns
were stationed at the entrance. Judd heard
one explain the process. "You're free to go sit
in your car, if you wish," the cop said. "But
don't start the engine until you see a clear
pathway to the exit ramp. So far only those
parked on levels one and two have even a
chance of getting out into the traffic jam

here, and you can see you're not going to get far anyway."

"I'm on level two," Judd told Vicki. "Maybe they've cleared the way for me."

The cop told everyone the elevators were not running, the pay booths were wide open, and that any looters or suspected car thieves would be shot on sight.

All over the multistory garage, workers labored to clear cars whose drivers had disappeared. Hundreds of cars had been coming into and leaving the garage when the Rapture had occurred. A little less than a quarter of those vehicles had been manned by people who were now gone. Their cars had continued until they struck other cars or walls, and there they sat, idling until they were out of gas.

Some of those cars had apparently had full tanks of gas, and if they were still running, workers were able to move them. The biggest job was finding a place for all those empty cars, just to get them out of the way. A long walkway snaked from the garage to the taxi-cab staging area, which was empty. All the cabs and cabbies swarmed the departure and arrival levels, seeking riders.

Of course, many of the cab drivers had disappeared as well. Fortunately, with so many others in the immediate area when that happened, this had resulted in just a bunch of fender benders. Other cabbies had grabbed those idling hacks and gotten them out of the way.

Judd shuddered as he and Vicki walked through the garage, passing cars with full suits of clothes in the driver's seat. He saw the occasional car with a stunned or weeping person who was sitting atop someone else's clothes, trying to maneuver the car out of the tangled mess.

Everywhere, workers were adding a gallon or two of gas to cars that had idled their fuel away. The workers all wore surgical gloves and masks, no one knowing what germs or diseases might have been left by whatever it was that had made these people disappear. Judd knew there was nothing to be afraid of, but he couldn't blame the emergency personnel for being careful.

At one end of the parking garage, a huge crane had been brought in, probably from a construction site at the airport. It was being used to lift cars over the guardrail and set them gently down in an area near the end of the garage.

When Judd found his father's car at the end of one row, he realized he was not in an advantageous position. Four cars blocked his, and in the row he would have to reach to get to the exit, workers were laboring over a gridlock of steel. A Chevy Blazer whose driver had disappeared had climbed one of the combination wood and steel parking guard-rails and hung itself up. It was still idling.

Judd carefully surveyed the situation. Four cars were lined up bumper to bumper from the wall at the end of the line where he had parked. They extended back past where he needed to back up.

"Vicki," he said, "do you think if we could get all four of those cars pushed back, I could get out of that parking spot?"

"I don't know," she said. "Let's walk it off and measure it."

There was a gap between the last of those four cars and a smashed up mess behind them. The question was, was the gap wide enough for all four cars? Measuring it with their steps, Judd and Vicki came to the con-clusion that there was room for the four cars, but not much room for Judd to back out. He would have to do it in several moves if he could do it at all. They had to try.

"We'll just have to take them one at a time," Judd said. He peered into the window of the last car in line. There were no clothes on the seat. The engine was off, but the keys were still in the ignition. "This must have been someone who panicked and ran off," he said. "Lucky for us they left their keys."

Judd started the engine and backed the car up as far as possible. He slowly maneuvered it until it tapped the first car in its way.

"The next car is still running!" Vicki shouted.

"Back it up here," Judd said.

"I've never driven," Vicki said. "You'd better do it."

Judd jogged up and opened the door, quickly realizing why Vicki didn't even want to try. This car was full of empty clothes. In the driver's seat was a woman's suit. Her shoes were on the floor. Atop the clothes were her glasses, necklace, earrings, and something that appeared to have fallen from her hair. As usual, Judd found dental fillings. On the floor, near the shoes, were the woman's watch and rings.

Judd smelled perfume. He held his breath. Not wanting to step on her belongings, he gathered them up and set them between the two front seats. On the passenger side, a man's suit and his belongings were draped where he had sat. Judd glanced in the backseat, where two people who had been sitting close had left everything but flesh and bone.

That gave Judd the willies, but he had to do what he had to do. He depressed the brake, shifted from drive into reverse, and backed the car out of the way.

The next car had its formerly lone occupant's clothes on the seat behind the wheel. Judd tossed these onto the passenger side and kicked the shoes out of the way. The car was in drive and the key was on, but it had run out of gas. "I'm gonna need your help here, Vicki," he said. "I'm going to shift this into neutral, then I'm gonna need you to steer it while I try to push it back into those other ones."

"I really don't want to be in that car with those clothes," Vicki said. "Anyway, I've never driven."

"This isn't driving," Judd said. "You'll just be keeping it straight until it touches that car back there."

"Please! I really don't want to do this."

"Well, what do you suggest? How are we going to get out of here if you don't help me?"

"Let me push," she said. "You steer."

"We can try," Judd said, "but I don't think you realize how heavy this car is."

"I'm pretty strong."

"Suit yourself. Try it."

Judd put the car in neutral, and Vicki climbed atop the hood. She put her feet on the trunk of the car ahead and wedged herself between the two cars. She pushed with all her might, trying to roll the car backward. It wouldn't budge. Judd opened the door and put his foot on the floor to help push that way. Nothing.

"I'm bigger than you are, Vicki. Let me try pushing while you steer."

"I told you I'm not getting in that car, and I'm not. Think of something else."

"There *is* nothing else. What are we supposed to do?"

"Just make sure the wheels are straight, Judd. Then we can both push. So what if it hits those cars back there? It's not going to move unless we both push it anyway."

Judd couldn't argue with that. Without the engine running, the power steering did not work. Straightening the wheels of that car was like driving a truck with no power steering at all. It took all of Judd's might to get the wheels to turn a couple of inches. He had to keep getting out to check whether they were lined up. When they were straight, he joined Vicki on the bumpers between the cars. With both of them putting their entire weight and muscle between the cars, the one finally began to slowly roll. Within seconds it had picked up a little speed, and Judd and Vicki dropped down from their perch on the second car. Judd ran to the driver's side and whipped open the door, feeling the tremendous weight and momentum of the vehicle. As it neared the car behind it, Judd jumped in. But before he could apply the brake or shift into park, the car smashed into the grille of the vehicle behind it.

Now there was barely enough room left between that car and the one pressed up against the wall near Judd's. What tricky problem might that offer?

Judd noticed that the front tires of the last car were turned sharply to the left. There were no clothes on the seat. No keys in the ignition. And the doors were locked. "This was obviously being driven by someone who had just started to turn left toward the exit when he was hit from behind by that other car."

"So he just left?" Vicki said.

"Wouldn't you have? You get hit by a car from behind and plow into the cement wall. You get out to see what happened and the car behind you gets hit and the car behind that one gets hit. There are no drivers in the middle two cars, only clothes. The driver of the last car runs off, leaving his keys in it. What would you do?"

"I guess I might turn mine off, take my keys, and lock my doors too," Vicki admitted.

"I'm going to have to break the window to get into this car," Judd said.

"I don't know much about cars," Vicki

said, "but what good will it do you to get into that car if the keys aren't there?"

"Good point," Judd said. "But somehow I've got to get this car out of the way if we're going to get out of this parking lot."

Judd and Vicki stood there surveying the situation and sizing up the possibilities.

"There's no way you're going to be able to back out of your space without at least clipping the bumper of that car," Vicki said. "Do you think your car could push that one out of the way a little bit? You'd still have a tough time backing out and getting around it, but it may be your only chance."

"No harm in trying," Judd said. "I can't think of anything else."

Judd told Vicki to line herself up near the crashed car and try to guide him with hand signals so he would come as close to missing it as possible. If he had to hit it, he'd hit it. If he had to hit it hard, he'd do that too. Whatever it took to push it out of the way, that was what he had to do.

Judd got into his car and started the engine. He looked in his rearview mirror and didn't see Vicki. He looked at the mirror on the door and saw her standing there, motioning him to start backing out. He pretended to busy himself with something else in the car on the seat. He had to stall. It wasn't that he didn't want to do this, it was just that he was suddenly overcome with a feeling of such sadness and loneliness and grief that he could barely move.

What was it about merely being inside the car with Vicki outside that made him feel so alone? It was almost as if he was in a trance. He still longed for this to be just a bad dream, but he knew it wasn't. He was tired. He wanted to lean over and put his head on the passenger seat and close his eyes. He fought tears. He fought drowsiness. He heard Vicki call out, "OK! OK, Judd!"

He waved and shifted into reverse. Judd slowly began to back out, carefully watching Vicki's signals. She made a circular motion with her index finger, and he turned the wheel. It was the wrong way. She quickly reversed the motion. He felt his car nudge the one next to him. He pulled back in and straightened out, taking another shot at it. This time he turned the other way and she signaled him until he was within inches of the crashed car behind him. He rolled down his window. "No way to clear it?" he asked.

"No way," she said.

"Let me get a line on it, then," he said. "I want to have the straightest shot at that bumper I can get in this small space."

"Back straight up from where you are then," Vicki said.

When Judd did, the bumper of his car finally nudged the car in the way. "I'm gonna go back up to the guardrail now," he said. "Let me know if I get out of line."

Judd edged forward slowly. At one point Vicki said, "Right, right, right." Judd feathered the steering wheel to the right. "Perfect," Vicki said. "As soon as you touch the guardrail, you're right in line."

"You'd better get out of the way, then," Judd said. "I'm going to have to ram it."

He waited until Vicki was clear. With his seat belt fastened, Judd took a deep breath, grimaced, and closed his eyes. He floored the accelerator.

With a squeal of tires, a crash, and a scraping, the blocking car was driven out of the way. Vicki yelped, and Judd didn't know if it was out of fear or excitement. Whichever, their little plan had succeeded, at least for the moment.

She jumped into the passenger's side and buckled herself in. Judd was able to back out of his parking space behind the car he had just pushed and would have to keep bumping it to give him room to get around it and head toward the exit. Once he did that, it appeared he had a fairly clear shot past the pay booths and into the gridlock of traffic that appeared to have moved hardly an inch since this whole ordeal had begun.

Vicki put her hand on Judd's arm. He stopped about six feet back of where emergency crews were still trying to extricate the idling Blazer from the guardrail. "It looks clear," Judd said. "I'm sure we can get past."

"I know," she said. "I just thought maybe we should thank God for helping us get out of here."

Judd nodded and bowed his head, wondering if she meant he should pray aloud, or she was going to, or what? When she said nothing, he began. "Lord, thanks. We didn't know what to—"

A nearly deafening engine roar and high-pitched squeal made Judd jump, and he looked up just in time to see workers diving out of the way of the Blazer. It had been lodged into the guardrail at a crazy angle, and apparently someone decided to set something on the accelerator and shift it into gear while others attempted to rock it free.

Whatever they had lodged against the gas pedal had made the engine race at top speed. Three wheels spun crazily, causing the screeching, but the fourth bit deep into the rail. The Blazer shuddered and shook, appearing as if it might explode. The tires sent smelly smoke everywhere.

As Judd and Vicki watched, the stuck tire somehow dislodged and sent the Blazer nose first into the low concrete ceiling with a horrific crash. All four wheels now burning rubber, the empty Blazer hit the floor, bouncing and careening into the cars around it.

The four-wheel-drive vehicle lurched directly in front of Judd, slammed the next guardrail, and flipped over forward, landing atop the last car he had moved. It drove the roof of that car all the way to the seat and rested atop the wreckage, tires still racing. The workers sprinted to the crash, and one reached in to turn off the engine.

Judd sat there with his mouth open. He turned to look at Vicki, whose eyes were wide and unblinking. "We could have been killed," she said. "If that had happened a couple of minutes ago, we would be dead for sure."

"Just think if we had gotten here earlier," Judd said, "and hadn't received Christ yet."

Now Judd knew exactly how to pray, and there was no awkwardness or wondering how to begin.

There was a certain sense of freedom in being able to drive even those few yards from the tangled garage and into the stalled traffic, but

Judd knew that they wouldn't be getting far very fast that night. To him, this traffic jam was just like his new life. He knew where he was going, but he had no idea how he was going to get there, or when.

FIVE

More Shocks

LIONEL awoke, terribly uncomfortable, about an hour before dawn. Ryan had provided him with a sleeping bag, but the Daleys' backyard, despite its manicured appearance, was hard and bumpy anyway. His back was sore, his whole body ached from the long bike ride, and he was still sad.

Lionel tried to pray. When he had been a phony, a kid in a Christian family who pretended to be like everyone else in the clan, it never surprised him that God seemed distant. He couldn't remember when God had seemed close. He knew that was because he had never become a true Christian, and that was also why he had been left behind.

But now shouldn't it be different? He knew God was real. He knew the Bible was true. And he knew for sure that when he had finally prayed to receive Christ—even though it was too late for him to be "caught up together in the clouds" with his family to meet Christ, as the Bible put it—God truly heard him. He felt forgiven, and he was sure he was saved. But his grief over the loss of his parents—though they were in heaven and not dead—and his horror over what had happened to Uncle André, plus the sheer exhaustion of trying to figure out what to do next, had caught up with him.

Whatever warm fuzzy feeling he might have hoped would go with his decision and his salvation had been covered over by his sense of regret and loss. And so he prayed. Just like before, it seemed his prayers were bouncing off the ceiling—or in this case, the canvas roof of the tent.

Lionel rolled onto his side and squinted at Ryan in the darkness. The little guy was sleeping soundly. At least he was sleeping deeply. Lionel had no idea whether it was really a sound sleep or not. What a horrible thing Ryan had been through. He didn't know what this was all about, but to him it had to look like something very spooky. It was one thing to be offered hope, to know you could still come to Christ and be saved for the future. But Ryan's parents had been killed and certainly didn't seem to have been Christians.

It was no wonder Ryan seemed angry, even angry with God. If all of what had happened was true, the way Bruce Barnes explained it—and Lionel knew it was—Ryan had to be drowning in confusion. What must he think of a God who would allow his parents to die and leave him behind while Christians disappeared into heaven?

Lionel's prayers to that point had been centered on himself. But now he found himself praying for other people. He knew it was hopeless to pray about something that had already happened, but he couldn't help pleading with God to assure him that maybe, just maybe, André had come to Christ before he was murdered or committed suicide. He even prayed the same thing for Ryan's parents. Was it possible someone could have been telling Mr. Daley about Christ just before the pilot of his plane disappeared, and could he have been saved just before they crashed?

Lionel knew that was a long shot, and he could never know anyway, but he could hope, couldn't he? And as long as he was hoping, maybe Mrs. Daley had had someone rush to her before she died and tell her about Jesus.

Lionel leaned on his elbow. He knew he

was hoping for too much. Quietly, he rolled over and stood, ducking to keep from hitting the top of the tent. He wanted to groan like his father did after sitting or lying in the same position for too long. But Lionel didn't want to wake Ryan. And anyway, he wasn't a middle-aged man. He was thirteen years old. There was no need to groan. He had simply overdone it, that was all.

Lionel moved to the flap and began unzipping it. He heard Ryan grunt and move, so he stopped and waited. An inch at a time, he carefully opened the flap and moved outside into the cool dew. He wanted to go to the bathroom, and there was nothing about Ryan's house that scared him. In fact, he wished Ryan would get over his fear so they could enjoy a little more comfort. He knew he would sleep better in the house, whether Ryan would or not.

Lionel tiptoed inside. After using the bathroom, he sat in the kitchen, staring at the photographs stuck to the refrigerator. Lionel hadn't known too many only children. Almost everybody he knew had at least one brother or sister, and most had more than that.

Lionel decided he would not have wanted to be an only child. Sure, there had to be advantages, but he would have missed knowing his older sister Clarice, the one he usually just called Reece. If ever there was someone who really lived out her faith, it was Reece. His mother and dad had been good Christians too, but it's hard to see only the good sides of your parents. His little brother and sister, Ronnie and Talia, had been great kids too, though they usually had gotten on his nerves.

It was Clarice who had almost made him a believer in time to be ready for the Rapture. She hadn't known he wasn't a Christian, of course. No one had, except André. And where was André now?

Clarice, with her sweet spirit and her prayer life, and the way her smile had seemed to sum up her whole life—she had been the best example of a Christian he knew. Maybe she had been too good an example. There had been times he knew he couldn't live up to her example, even if he had been a Christian. Now he knew how dumb he had been. He knew better. He knew he wasn't supposed to live up to anything. He was just supposed to trust Christ and be thankful for the gift of salvation. But it was a gift he had never received.

Lionel noticed Mr. Ryan's sales awards. Those didn't mean much now. Ryan might have been proud of his dad, but whatever he had done and however he had been rewarded, that hadn't helped him when the end came.

Lionel moseyed back outside and began unzipping the tent flap again. He heard Ryan gasp. "Lionel! Someone's trying to get in!"

"It's just me, Ryan. I was inside."

"Oh! You scared me!"

"Sorry. It was just getting too close in here."

"I'm not going to be able to stand staying in this tent, Lionel. But I can't go into my house either. It's like a nightmare, like I can't even force myself to go through the door. Does your house feel that way to you?"

"Sort of, but I think I'll get over it. I mean, those clothes give me the creeps, but maybe if I just gathered 'em up and put 'em away, it wouldn't be so bad. I think one night in this tent is enough for me too. You wanna just go to my place now?"

"I was hoping you'd say that."

It was still dark when Ryan and Lionel packed their stuff in backpacks and rode off toward Lionel's. They both skidded to a stop two blocks from Lionel's house several minutes later, just as it came into view. A beat up old car was parked out front, next to a late-model van, and men were moving in and out of the house.

"Who are they?" Ryan asked.

"I have no idea," Lionel said, his heart thumping. "Let's get closer without letting them see us."

He and Ryan took a left and circled around the back way. "I wonder if they're looters," Lionel whispered when they dismounted and came toward the house from the back.

"Robbing your house?" Ryan said. "That's happening a lot."

"I can't let 'em do it," Lionel said.

"There are a lot of them and only one of you."

"There are two of us, Ryan."

"Don't get me in on this. This isn't my fight."

"What're you now, a chicken? I would have defended your house against looters. You want 'em to clean me out?"

"What do I care? It's not my place."

"Some kind of a friend you are."

"I never said I was your friend, Lionel."

Lionel stopped and stared at Ryan. What was this all of a sudden? "Oh, I get it," he said. "I'm fine as long as I'm keeping you company and giving you something to think about besides yourself and your parents. But as soon as I need you to help me a little, you're done with me."

"I'm only saying we just met, Lionel. Don't

go thinking I'm your best friend who's going to be with you through everything."

"Believe me, Ryan, I'll never make that mistake again. Why don't you ride on home and stay in your tent until you're brave enough to go in the house."

"Stop it! That's not fair!"

"Face it, Ryan, you're a coward."

"What're you gonna do, Lionel? Take on these guys by yourself?"

"Looks like I might have to. This is my house. I can't let people walk off with our stuff."

"I'll stay here and be ready to call for help if you need it."

"Well, I sure hope no one sneaks up behind you and says *boo!*"

Ryan crouched in the alley, shaking his head. Lionel crept toward the house.

Just before dawn, Judd Thompson Jr. pulled into the trailer park where Vicki Byrne lived. It was a good thing they had talked all night in the heavy stop-and-go traffic all the way from O'Hare to Mount Prospect, because she was sleeping now. Judd didn't have to wake her after getting directions to her place.

He couldn't remember having been somewhere like this before. He had an uncle who
had lived in a trailer when Judd was a very
small boy, but his recollections of the place
were vague. He remembered his uncle more
than his uncle's trailer. He certainly didn't
remember it being as run-down as the ones
in this park, and he would have been a
scared little kid if he had seen the rough
characters then that he was seeing now. They
were shirtless, tattooed, scowling bearded
men and hard-looking women who appeared
as if they would just as soon smack you as
look at you.

One of the black leather–clad men stepped
in front of Judd's car and slammed both
palms on the hood. "Where do you think
you're goin', boy!"

Judd hit the brake and rolled his window
down a couple of inches. He was so scared
he could hardly speak. Fortunately, he didn't
have to. "Wait, Judd!" Vicki said, roused by
the noise. "I know this guy!" She leaned
across Judd and rolled his window all the
way down. "What's going on, Vince?"

"What's going on?" he repeated. "You
don't know what's going on? Where you
been?"

"With a friend. Now what's up?"

"Well, while we were sleeping, somebody

came through here and looted and burned all the trailers where nobody was home. Some of the trailers are trashed, and some of 'em are burned to the ground."

"What about ours?"

"You don't want to know."

"Yes I do! Now what?"

"Burned, Vick. I'm sorry. You know if we'd a seen anybody, we'd a killed 'em."

"I know you would."

"So, where are your people?"

"Disappeared, Vince."

Vince stepped back and ran his hand through his hair. "Wow! No kiddin'! What about your brother up north?"

"Gone too."

"You're sure?"

"Yup. Totally. I'm the only one left."

"What do you make of this, Vicki? You're not buyin' that this is all God's doing, are you?"

"As a matter of fact I am, Vince. Look around. Look who's missing. What else could it be?"

"I sure hope you're wrong."

"I hope I'm not. Can we get back there and see the trailer?"

"Probably. There's not much to see. You sure you want to?"

"I want to."

"Take it easy."

Vince backed out of the way and waved Judd on. "Let this guy through!" Vince hollered. "Leave this car alone! It's Vicki and a friend!"

As Judd carefully maneuvered his way through the water and mud and debris, people along the asphalt drive and walkways approached the car with sad faces and sorrowful comments to Vicki. "We're sorry, sweetheart," they said. "You can stay with us. Call us. Come for dinner. We'll help you."

Vicki waved her thanks at each person and showed Judd where to drive. When what was left of the Byrne family trailer came into view, she gasped. Judd couldn't even make out the color of the accents or the trim. The trailer was just a pile of twisted, smoking, blistered metal now. Its tires were flat and melted, only the stabilizing bar and bricks still recognizable.

Vicki lowered her head and sobbed as the crowd that had gathered around the trailer slowly moved away, seeming to Judd to want to leave Vicki to her own grief. He had heard her story. He knew she would not have felt any emotional attachment to this place before. But what must it now represent for her? She had grown up here, rebelled against her parents here, broken their curfew here.

She had learned to smoke and drink and run with a bad crowd. And though she had hated it, she had seen her parents and her brother and sister come to Christ in this little home. Now they were gone, she was alone, and the trailer was no more.

At least, Judd thought, *she knows the truth now.*

SIX

Showdown

LIONEL Washington could barely breathe as he sneaked up to the driveway at the side of his own house. He peered into the basement window where he and his uncle André had shared the foldout couch just two nights before, the night of the vanishings all over the world.

Someone appeared to be setting up housekeeping down there. Lionel saw boxes of food, piles of strange clothes, a fan, a clock, a small bedside stand. Who thought they were free to move into his house, just because the rest of his family was gone? He thought he would find people taking stuff away, not moving stuff in.

Two men about Lionel's uncle's age burst from the door in a trot, heading toward the van. Lionel was startled but scampered back to behind the corner of the house before they noticed him. "This is going to be great," one of them said. "This is a good way for André to work off his debt."

"You gonna let him stay here?"

The other laughed. "He's the one who put us onto this place, man! 'Course he can stay here. Long as he behaves himself."

They were both laughing now as the door slapped shut behind them. While they were busy in the van, Lionel slipped into the house and up the stairs. Three or four other people were inside, but they ignored him. What was this, anyway?

Clearly, these people were moving in, taking over the house as if it were their own. The piles of clothes that had been the only remaining evidence of the other members of Lionel's family had already been gathered up and put somewhere. Lionel bounded down the stairs to see if his father's pajamas and robe and slippers were gone too.

At the bottom of the stairs he was met by the two who had gone out to the van. He recognized them as André's so-called friends, the ones he said he owed money. "Well, if it ain't the nephew!" the taller one said. "What's your name again?"

Lionel was not as brave as he tried to sound. "My name's Washington, and this is my house."

"Is it now? You own this place?"

"My family does."

"But your family is gone, ain't it?"

"So what?"

"So you need someone to look out for you and take care of the place, and that's what we're going to do for you. And no charge."

"Says who?"

"Says us, punk, so watch your mouth. André told us everybody but you disappeared from this place. He's got seniority in the family now."

"What's that mean?"

"That means of the only two people left who can claim this place, he's the oldest. I mean, he is older than you, ain't he?"

"'Course."

"Well, there you go."

"So where *is* my uncle André?"

"He's around."

"How do you know?"

"He owes us money, that's how we know. He'll show up here, and he'll let us stay until he pays. We know he'll never pay. Why should he? This is the best deal for him and for us."

Lionel wanted to ask them what they would say if he told them André was dead. But he didn't want to give that away yet. When he said nothing, the shorter guy said, "Don't worry, little dude. You can stay here too. Just stay out of our way and keep your mouth shut."

"In my own house?"

"You'd better get used to the fact that this is not your house anymore, kid."

"What if I call the police?"

"You think the police have time to worry about you right now? We could kill you and bury you and leave a pile of your clothes on a chair, and they'd believe you were one of those people who disappeared. Trust me, boy, you're better off with a place to stay. We'll even let you eat, maybe teach you the business."

"The business?"

"The business of makin' money, son."

"Crime, you mean?"

"To some people. To us it's business. You can get in on the ground floor. What do you say?"

Lionel was afraid of what they might do if he tried to kick them out. He didn't want them to know he had no intention of staying with them. He just shrugged and trotted back upstairs. He filled his dad's old canvas duffel bag with everything—and more than—he thought he'd ever need, and he lugged it downstairs.

"Pick your own place to crash, dude," the taller one said. "After all, this *was* your house."

"It still is!" Lionel yelled as he ran past them and out the door. He was shocked that they ignored him. No one even tried to catch him as he raced down the driveway, into the alley, and back toward the bikes, where he hoped Ryan was standing guard. The bikes were there. Ryan wasn't.

"Wait here, please," Vicki Byrne told Judd. She stepped out of the car and stood staring at the pile of rubble that had once been her home. She was puzzled at her own reaction. How she had once hated this place! It was too small, too dingy. It told the world she was poor, that her family was of little account, that she was trailer trash.

That very trailer had made her resent people who lived in normal homes, let alone rich people who lived in large houses. She had assumed all kinds of evil things about people who seemed above her in society. She didn't know if it was true that they were mean and nasty and selfish, but it made her feel a little better to think they were not worthy of whatever they had and she didn't.

But now, as she stood in the cool of the morning, staring at the slowly rising smoke

and smelling the acrid fumes, she was overcome with a longing for that little trailer
house. She remembered how it looked, how
it smelled, how it creaked when she walked
through it. She had even learned where to
step to keep from making noise when she
tried to sneak in after curfew.

That seemed so long ago now, but it had
been just two nights before that she thought
she had gotten away with something. She
had sneaked in late and thought her parents
were asleep. Only later did she realize that
they and her little sister and her big brother
in Michigan had been among those who had
disappeared before midnight Chicago time.

Was it only her realization that they had
been right about God that made her feel sen-
timental toward a place she used to hate? Or
was it just her fatigue and grief over the loss
of her family that put them in a new light?
She knew it was all that and more. She had
finally come to see that she had been wrong
about God. She knew she had been a sinner
and that she needed him. And when she had
committed her life to him, he began right
away to change how she felt about things.
She saw what a fool she had been, what an
ungrateful rebel. How could she have been
so blind? What had been her problem?

She had not wanted to admit that her parents had really changed, but it was obvious to everyone, herself included. She had been so determined to hang on, to control her own life, that she refused to let anyone know she even noticed the difference. That was what hurt her the most as she gazed at the remains of everything she owned except the clothes she was wearing.

What a strange feeling that was, knowing she would have to start over from scratch. No clothes. No belongings. No nothing.

She turned slowly and moved back toward Judd's car. She had never hung with anyone who drove such a nice car, certainly not a sixteen-year-old. So far Judd had seemed to fit the rich-kid mold she had imagined, but there were good and nice and kind parts to him too. And like he had said, they were now brother and sister in Christ. She'd better learn to like and trust him, she decided. With not a possession to her name, she was probably going to have to depend on him for a while.

"Are you all right?" he asked when she slid back into the car.

She shrugged. "I guess. I'm not sure what else can go wrong."

"You're going to have to stay with me, you know," he said.

"Oh, Judd, I couldn't expect you to do that for me."

"I'd give you your privacy and everything. I mean, I wouldn't take advantage or do anything wrong or—"

"I know. But I just couldn't—"

"Sure you could. You have no choice."

"Someone here will give me a place to stay."

"No, no I insist. I have money and credit cards. My dad has some bank accounts, and I know he'd want me to use them to survive."

"Judd, it doesn't make sense."

"Of course it does. You need clothes, stuff, a place to live, food."

"But why should I expect that from you?"

"You think God is going to take care of you?"

"Now's the best time to find out," she said.

"Well, I'm how he's going to do it." Judd pulled slowly out of the trailer park.

"You're what? And where are you going?"

"I'm what God will use to take care of you. You're a Christian now, and he's going to watch over you and make sure you're taken care of. He's going to use me to do that."

"So you're God's guy now, his right hand man?"

"You could say that."

"So, where are we going?"

"To my house."

"Judd!"

"Just let me do this, Vicki. I really think God wants me to, and I'll feel like I'm letting him down if I don't."

Vicki found that hard to argue with. Maybe she *was* supposed to let Judd do this. Maybe this really *was* God's way of providing for her. "But if we stay in the same house, won't we get tired of each other and start hating each other?"

"I doubt it," Judd said, and Vicki was surprised. She really wasn't sure what she thought of this guy. He was not her type, and she probably never would have given him a second glance before. But he was being nice now. And that had been a nice thing to say, that he doubted he would get tired of her.

But he didn't know her either. He didn't know how she could be. She was independent and crabby and grouchy and self-centered. At least she *had* been that way. Could it be that those were things God would start to change in her? Or would she have the same personality and character, but just be a Christian now? She wasn't sure how it all worked, but she knew her parents had seemed different almost overnight.

She felt different; she knew that. Even with the fear and the dread of having lost everyone close to her in an instant, she found herself thinking of other people. Not every second, and not every time. But in just the few short hours she had lived since deciding to become a Christian, she noticed some changes.

"I'll check it out," she told Judd. "I'll see where you live and see if it would work for a short time. But I don't plan on being in your way for long. And I can't be sure it would work out at all."

Judd nodded. Vicki could tell he wanted it to work. But maybe he was just afraid to be alone. That was all right. So was she. It would be good to have someone to talk to.

"I'll tell you one thing," she said, as Judd drove toward his house, "I'm starving and I'm exhausted. If you've got any food and a place for me to sleep, I'll take it."

"Coming right up," Judd said.

Ryan Daley had panicked. He had stayed close enough to keep an eye on Lionel until Lionel had sneaked into the house. Ryan was sure Lionel would get himself kidnapped or shot or something, and then what would Ryan do? He felt like such a coward, trying to get out of doing anything dangerous. But he had just lost his parents. How was he supposed to feel brave all of a sudden?

Ryan had crouched behind a neighbor's garage with his and Lionel's bikes. He didn't know what he would do if Lionel called for help, but he stayed out of sight and ready anyway. He was startled when Lionel went in the house when the two older guys came out to get something from the van. When they went back in, Ryan was sure Lionel was in big trouble. When he didn't come out for a while—and neither did the older two—Ryan was convinced something awful had happened.

Then there came Lionel, bounding out of the house with a big duffel bag over his shoulder. Ryan convinced himself that Lionel could be running only because someone was after him. A stranger. A bad guy. Someone with a knife or a gun. And Lionel was leading whoever that was right to Ryan. He didn't even take the time to mount his bike. He just ran off as fast as he could.

He had been doing a lot of that lately.

SEVEN

Crises

VICKI felt awkward when Judd pulled into the driveway of his big suburban home. She had been in a house that size only twice before, both times for parties. She hadn't felt comfortable then either. But this was different. There was no party here. There was no one here but the two of them. When was the last time she had been alone with a teenage boy without winding up drinking, smoking, doing dope, or worse?

Judd seemed nervous, showing her around, telling her she could stay in the guest bedroom downstairs while he would keep his room upstairs. "Doesn't it give you the creeps to stay so close to where the rest of your family used to be?" she asked.

"A little," he said. "But I have no choice. Where else would I go?"

Vicki had just been thinking the same thing. She didn't say so. All she said was, "I hate to ask, but do you have anything to eat around here?"

"Name it," Judd said. "We have anything and everything you want."

Vicki and Judd raided the refrigerator and ate well. She noticed he was as heavy-eyed as she was. "I don't like to sleep during the day," she said. "But I'm going to pass out sitting here if I don't lie down."

Judd pointed to the guest room. "I'm going to sleep too," he said. "I wouldn't be surprised if I sleep all day and all night, but I've never done that before. More likely, I'll wake up after seven or eight hours, like I always do."

"Me too," she said. "But I don't remember ever being so exhausted."

"I'd say we've been through a lot, wouldn't you?" he said.

They both laughed for the first time since they'd known each other.

Vicki quickly grew serious. She said, "You know, Judd, I'm going to have to ask you to run me somewhere tomorrow so I can get some clothes. I'll keep track of whatever it costs and pay you back."

"No problem," he said, "but first you

ought to check my mom's closet. She was about your size."

"Really? What size was she?"

"I don't know. She was about your size, that's all I know."

"Wow," Vicki said. "I hope I'm still thin when I'm her age."

"If you believe what Bruce Barnes believes, we haven't got much more than seven years to live anyway."

"Plenty of time to get fat," Vicki said, shrugging. What kind of a remark was that? She had never engaged in small talk with anyone before. In the past everything she talked about had been centered on what she liked or didn't like, what she was going to do or not do. She hated talking about normal things—"nothing" things, she always called them. This was the stuff adults and other boring types always talked about.

"You can have whatever you want of my mom's stuff," Judd said. "I mean, she's obviously not coming back. Will it make you feel weird?"

"Weird?"

"Wearing someone else's clothes, someone who disappeared."

"How will you feel seeing me in your mom's clothes?"

"I don't guess I'd mind. You'll probably

wear them differently—I mean, tied up or cut off or tucked in or untucked or whatever."

"Yeah, and I hope it will be temporary anyway. I want to get a job and get myself some new stuff."

"Sure. But meanwhile . . ."

"Meanwhile I'll try to get by if there's anything that works, so I won't have to wear dirty clothes."

"Good. You want to look for some stuff now, in case you want to change when you get up? I mean, you don't have to. You look perfectly fine, but you might want some fresh . . . not that what you're wearing doesn't look fresh or anything, but—"

"It's all right, Judd. Yes, I would like to see if there's something I could wear when I wake up. Did your mother wear jeans, sweaters, that kind of stuff, or only dresses and old ladies' stuff?"

"Here's a picture of her."

Vicki studied the photograph of a very youthful, trim, and definitely petite woman. "Is this a recent picture?"

"Yeah."

"She looks very stylish."

"My friends said she was a babe."

"To her face?"

"No, to mine. I was proud of her."

Judd was talking about his mother as if she

were dead. It seemed to Vicki his voice was about to break.

"I can see why you were proud of her," Vicki said. "If she has a lot of clothes like this, I'd be honored to wear them. Remember, Judd, she's not dead. If everything we believe is true, and we both know it is, she's in heaven."

"I know," he said, sitting on the couch and sighing. "But she might as well be dead. She's dead to me. I won't see her again."

"Not here, anyway," Vicki agreed, "but in heaven or when Jesus comes back."

"I guess I wouldn't want to see her in heaven," Judd said. "That would mean I'd have to die within the next seven years."

"Not necessarily," Vicki said, yawning. "Bruce says the seven last years don't actually begin until Israel signs some sort of a treaty with that Antichrist guy."

Again Vicki was stunned at what was coming out of her own mouth. Would she have heard of or known any of this a week ago? Would she have cared? Would she have talked about it? Hardly. She had never cared about politics, especially international politics. She didn't really care about much outside her own trailer park. Now not only was life in the park gone, but she also was talking about global affairs with a rich kid she had just met.

"Nobody even knows if the Antichrist is around yet," Judd said. "But Bruce said he already has his eye on somebody."

"I don't think I'd even want to know who it was," Vicki said.

"I sure do," Judd said. "I don't want to be sucked in by him and fooled."

"Well, that's true."

"You want to look at those clothes now?"

"Sure. Then I'm getting some sleep."

Judd directed her to his parents' bedroom and left Vicki to look around in there for herself. She found it eerie. Not forty-eight hours earlier, people were living here with no idea their minutes were numbered. It was a neat room, but stuff was left about, the way it is when people think they'll be back to tidy up. A jewelry box was open. A drawer was half shut. One side of the closet was open, the other shut. Books were on the nightstands; half a glass of water was on the floor next to the bed.

Vicki was so tired she could barely keep her eyes open. She checked the closet and wondered what it must be like to have the money to live this way. Judd's mom's closet looked like a department store. Shoes, slacks, blouses, blazers, dresses, belts, you name it.

She had been serious when she'd said Judd's mom looked stylish, but these kinds of things had never been her style. She had favored a hotter look, a street look, lots of black and leather.

Vicki pulled out a pantsuit that looked way too old for her, but she imagined it with the top untucked and the blazer open. She held it against her body and looked in the mirror on the back of the bedroom door.

Vicki was startled by her own appearance. She took two steps backward and sat on the bed, the hangered pantsuit still pressed against her. She stared at her greasy hair, her makeupless face, her puffy eyes. When was the last time she had paid attention to her face without a load of makeup and mascara? She looked old and tired, yet her youthfulness peeked through too. The girl in the mirror looked scared, tired, haggard. She had for so long hidden that little girl, trying to make herself appear older. Maybe it had worked, but she didn't want to appear older now. She wanted to be who she was, a four-teen-year-old girl who had finally come face-to-face with God. Finally she knew who he was and what he was about. She had given herself to him when she looked just like this, and she didn't want to change.

Sure, she hoped she looked better when

she had had a little sleep and a shower and clean hair. But she was finished trying to look like a woman in her twenties. No more hiding. No more pretending to be something she wasn't. She would wear an older woman's clothes, but she would wear them in such a way that she was honest with herself, with others, and with God. She was a teenager who had been left behind, but she was also one who had seen what was right and acted upon it. She belonged to God now, and she would present herself to him as she really was.

There was nothing wrong with looking nice, but she no longer felt the need to look hard, or sexy, or old. She lay back on the bed and stared at the ceiling, Mrs. Thompson's pantsuit draped over her. In a minute, she decided, she would get up and head for the guest room. But within seconds she had drifted into a deep, deep sleep.

Ryan Daley dove behind a hedge across the street and a block behind Lionel's house. Lionel came charging by, muttering, "Where are you, you little chicken?"

"I'm right here," Ryan answered.

Lionel skidded to a stop and glared at Ryan. "You *are* a chicken!" he said. "Look at you! Hiding there like a little scared rabbit."

"So, what am I, a chicken or a rabbit?"

Lionel shook his head, looking disgusted. Ryan found it hard to believe this boy was only a year older than he was. Lionel seemed so much older, so much more mature. He seemed like the kind of guy who could get along on his own, who would stand up to bad guys like he had apparently just done. Ryan couldn't imagine ever doing something like that.

"We've got to get back there and get our bikes," Lionel said. "Where'd you run off to, anyway?"

"What do you mean?" Ryan said. "You can see where I ran off to. I'm right here, aren't I?"

"I mean *why* did you run off?"

"Because I saw you being chased."

"No one was chasing me."

"Why were you running then?"

"I figured if I surprised them by bolting out of there, I'd have a big enough head start that they'd give up before they started. They must have."

"But, Lionel, they'll get us when we go back for the bikes."

"You want to walk all the way to your house?"

"My house? I thought we were going to stay here!"

Lionel sighed and told Ryan the story. "So I don't think we're staying here until I can get the police to throw them out."

"So call the police."

"Maybe I will. But don't you think they have enough to worry about right now, without trying to figure out who owns my house and who should be there or shouldn't? I mean, if the cops find out I'm thirteen and the only one left in my family, they'll try to put me in some orphanage or something."

"Orphanage?" Ryan repeated. No way. He had never heard anything good about an orphanage. Talk about a nightmare. Worst of all, when he thought about it, he realized that now he *was* an orphan. Being abandoned by his parents had always been his biggest fear, and he didn't think that was just because he was an only child. He was sure he would have felt that way even if he had had brothers and sisters, and that made him wonder if Lionel felt the same. He had to, didn't he? But he believed this was all about Jesus and heaven and everything, so maybe Lionel was handling it better. At least that's the way it seemed to Ryan.

Lionel also seemed more interested in getting their bikes. "I want my bike too," Ryan said, "but I'm still not going inside my house."

"Man, you've *got* to get over that," Lionel said. "You can't sleep in a tent the rest of your life, and I know *I'm* not going to."

"I just can't go in my house," Ryan said. "What are we going to do?"

"We're going to start by getting our bikes. Now come on."

Lionel left his duffel bag in the bushes, and Ryan followed him as he crept back toward his house. The two guys who knew André were still casually going in and coming out of the house, unloading stuff from their van. Lionel said, "Let's wait until they've just carried some stuff in, then we can run up, get our bikes, and speed away."

"And what if they see us and come after us in that car or that van?"

"What if Chicken Little was right and the sky falls in?" Lionel said. "You've got to learn to take some chances, man."

Ryan figured that was supposed to be funny, but he didn't laugh. Lionel was making him feel like a wuss. He had never felt that way before. He was an athlete, a tough guy. Kids looked up to him, respected him. What would they think of him now, running away and hiding?

But how was he supposed to act? The

worst thing that could happen to a kid had happened to him. His parents were dead and gone, and he had no one left. Anytime anything bad had happened in his life before, his parents had been there for him. When his dad was gone to some sales training school for three months one time, his mother had been there. When she was in the hospital for back surgery, his dad had been there. Neither could do everything the other had always done with him and for him, but they tried. And they had made do until the other parent was home and back into the routine.

But what was he supposed to do now? Both parents were gone, and he couldn't talk to either of them about the loss of the other. He felt alone in the world. He really didn't want to irritate Lionel. If he lost this friend too, where would he be?

"OK," Ryan said finally. "When they go in the house, they've been staying inside for a couple minutes before they come back out. As soon as the screen door slams behind them, we go. That should give us enough time."

Lionel looked at him, and Ryan thought he actually detected admiration, or at least respect, on his face. "All right," Lionel said. "Now you're thinking. Let's go."

They crouched behind a corner of the

house and peered at the door. The two came out, laughing and joking. "Too easy, man," one said. "This is too easy. Easy and sweet. Wait till André gets here."

From the front, Ryan heard the two grunting as they dragged something heavy from the van. "That's the last of it, then?" he heard.

"Yup, that's all. Set it down a second so I can kick that door shut."

Ryan heard the sound of the van door closing. Lionel and Ryan peeked out as the two lugged a small couch up to the door at the side of the house. The two fumbled with the door, finally hollering inside for "one of you lazy slobs to get this door for us!"

A young woman came running. "Just ask, you two. I'm here and I'm not lazy!"

They moved into the house with the couch, and the screen door slapped shut behind them. Lionel took off like a shot, and Ryan was right behind him. Fast as he had been for years, he couldn't keep up with Lionel. Lionel must have been really scared or really fast because he was moving like the wind.

They reached the bikes, and Lionel was quickly up on his and riding off in the direction of his hidden duffel bag. Ryan saw his own big bag on the ground next to his bike and considered leaving it right there. How would he handle it and ride fast too? But he couldn't leave it. He needed everything in there. And besides, those guys weren't even coming back out to the van, were they? Hadn't they said that was all of it?

Ryan bent to grab the bag and slowly mounted his bike, hoping to make no noise or draw any attention to himself. He had to keep one foot on the ground for balance as he slowly wobbled off, and once he had to come to a full stop to shift the weight of the bag. Just as he was starting to gain a little momentum, that scary, tingly feeling of fear raced up and down his back. Lionel was reaching down to grab his own bag from the bushes a block away, but Ryan was sure he heard footsteps and shouting behind him.

EIGHT

Taking Flight

Judd found himself shy and embarrassed about having a girl in his house when he was alone. He had dated before, of course, but his parents had put such restrictions on him that he had pretty much given up asking girls out. He saw them at school and after school, but he didn't have one special girl.

He was curious, of course, about who would be there and who would have disappeared when school began again. And who knew when that might be? A few days ago he wouldn't have cared if he never went to school again. Now he wondered, if Bruce Barnes was right about the Rapture signaling the end of the world in about seven years, whether school was worth anything. If it was true that the Antichrist, whomever that was, might soon sign some sort of an agreement with Israel, the seven years would begin, and Jesus would return again before Judd turned twenty-four.

While that might have convinced him that he didn't have a whole life and career to study for, he also realized how much time he had wasted in school already. For as old as he was and the grade he was in, he felt he hardly knew anything. Maybe it would be all right for school to start up again, once this traffic and fire and death mess had been cleaned up. Then he would try to learn as much as he could, at least about the basics, so he would be able to get along on his own for the rest of the time.

If all this was true, Judd felt obligated to serve God by telling others that they still had a chance. There was certainly no reason to pursue a big moneymaking career. He may have never before had a goal, a purpose, a reason for doing anything other than pleasing himself, but he sure did now. True, this had been thrust upon him. He'd had little choice. Of course, he could have chosen to ignore God, to thumb his nose at the Creator and continue living for himself. But he had been a rebel, not an ignoramus. Clearly, God had convinced him of the truth, and now Judd had made the decision himself. He had a lot of pain and grief and regret to work

through, but from now on, it was he and
God all the way.

Judd waited politely for Vicki to emerge
from his parents' bedroom. He wanted to tell
her she could feel free to use the shower in
the master bath. When she shut the door
almost all the way, he assumed she might be
trying on something in front of the mirror.
He didn't want to walk in on her.

But she didn't come out, and he heard no
water running. He looked at his watch and
decided that in five minutes he would dis-
cretely knock, tell her about the shower, and
finally be able to get upstairs to collapse in
his own bed. He sat on the couch and clicked
on the television to check the progress of the
massive cleanup. Then he decided to call
Bruce Barnes and see if he and Vicki could
come by that evening or the next morning,
whenever they woke up, to tell him some
news. Judd was sure Bruce would be thrilled
that they had made their decisions. Also, he
wanted to know where he might find those
other two kids, Lionel and Ryan. It seemed
they were all in this together and that they
should watch out for each other.

Judd muted the TV and dialed the church.
He reached an answering machine with
Bruce's voice on the greeting. Bruce sounded
as shocked as anybody. This must've been a

message he recorded within a couple of hours of the Rapture.

The message said: "You have reached New Hope Village Church. We are planning a weekly Bible study, but for the time being we will meet just once each Sunday at 10 A.M. While our entire staff, except me, and most of our congregation are gone, the few of us left are maintaining the building and distributing a videotape our senior pastor prepared for such a time as this. You may come by the church office anytime to pick up a free copy, and we look forward to seeing you Sunday morning."

Judd did not leave a message, figuring he'd call back after Vicki finished showering. He looked down the hall toward his parents' room. He heard nothing and the door was still nearly closed. He began to get up and head that way when he noticed bizarre images on the TV screen. He sat back down and turned the sound up.

Breathless CNN announcers told strange stories from around the world as they showed videotaped images of people disappearing right out of their clothes. A husband videotaping his wife about to give birth caught the nurse's uniform floating to the ground and his wife's huge stomach going suddenly flat. The baby had disappeared.

Local TV stations from around the world had submitted tapes of disappearances where the vanishings had occurred in time zones where it was daytime. Judd watched, fascinated, as a groom disappeared while placing the wedding ring on his bride's finger. A funeral home in Australia reported that nearly all the mourners and the corpse had disappeared from one funeral. At the same funeral home in another funeral at the same time, only a few mourners disappeared and the corpse remained.

A video cameraman caught the action at a cemetery as three pallbearers disappeared and the other three dropped the casket, which broke open to reveal it was empty. The video panned to several freshly opened graves with bodies suddenly missing. The CNN anchorman announced that morgues all over the world reported various numbers of bodies missing.

At a soccer game between two missionary schools in Indonesia, a parent had videotaped all but one player disappearing right from their uniforms during play. The announcer said that that one remaining player had reportedly taken his own life in his remorse over the loss of his friends. Judd knew better. Judd could have been that player. That suicide was the result of despair, not of remorse. That kid knew where his friends were and knew he had missed his chance. The problem was, no one had told him he had another chance.

When the TV moved on to more mundane reports of the cleanup, of a Romanian leader planning to visit the United Nations, and of a word of comfort and encouragement from United States President Gerald Fitzhugh, Judd fought to keep his eyes open. He lay on his side on the couch, wondering if he should call out for Vicki to see if she wanted to watch any of the disappearances if they were shown again. Within minutes, with the TV droning, Judd was out. He would sleep, motionless, for hours.

Ryan Daley had been wrong about hearing something behind him. His imagination was playing such tricks on him that he was sure he heard footsteps and shouting and was certain someone was gaining on him, someone who might yank him right off his bike.

He was already wrestling with his heavy bag in one hand and trying to steer with the other while keeping his balance. When he wrenched around to see who was about to nab him, the motion threw him completely off-kilter. He was relieved to see no one there, but as he turned back to face the front, he was wobbling and careening toward the corner of a garage. He frantically jerked the handlebars the other way, which pitched him and his bag off the bike and into the side of the garage. He bounced and rolled up and over the bike and onto his head. A pedal punched a deep bruise into his side, and his forehead was scraped.

Mostly, Ryan felt stupid. He had been knocked off his bike and injured by absolutely no one. He glanced back at Lionel's house. All those trespassing creeps were inside. They didn't care a whit about Ryan or Lionel or what they were up to.

Slowly, painfully, Ryan remounted his bike and pedaled off, looking for Lionel. Lionel was riding in a circle in the street a block away, waiting. "Why didn't you come for me, man?" Ryan complained. "They could have had me!"

"But they didn't, did they? I looked back just as you were looking back, and I saw what you saw. Nobody. Too bad you didn't learn to ride without running into garages."

Ryan figured Lionel was only teasing him, but he wasn't in the mood for it and it made him mad. In fact, he felt more angry than he had in a long time. Ryan had been known to be a bit of a hothead in sports when things didn't go his way. And he could scream and yell at Raymie Steele and his other friends once in a while. But he felt such a rage at Lionel that he could hardly contain himself. He wanted to kill this kid, despite the fact that right then Lionel was the last friend Ryan had in the world—at least that he knew of.

Ryan imagined himself jumping off his bike and charging Lionel, knocking him off his own bike and pounding him into the ground. He wondered if Lionel knew what he was thinking, because Lionel looked strangely at Ryan, as if he was worried about him.

"Are you OK, man?" Lionel asked.

"Of course I'm not OK!" Ryan shot back. "How could I be OK? My parents are dead, I don't believe in God—at least a God who would do this—and I have nowhere to live! How could I be OK?"

"You've got a place to live," Lionel said. "*I'm* the one without a house. You just have to get over your fear and talk yourself into going inside. What do you think, that death is contagious or something? You'll be safer in your own house than any other place I can think of."

"I just can't, Lionel. Now don't pressure me."

"Well, anyway, what I really meant was are

you OK with that scrape on your forehead? You need to get that cleaned and bandaged."

"Where are we going to do that?"

"At your house. Follow me."

"Lionel!"

"You don't have to go in, you big baby. I'll get the stuff and do it in the driveway. But I might try to get you inside if you'll let me."

"I want to go inside, but I can't."

"Let's worry about that when we get there."

"Don't try to make me do something I'm not ready for, Lionel."

When they arrived several minutes later, Ryan waited in the driveway while Lionel went in through the back. When he came out with a first-aid kit, Ryan thought he was strangely silent. "What's the matter?" Ryan asked.

"You don't wanna know."

"'Course I do. What's up?"

"I'll never get you in there now."

"Why?"

"Just hush up and hold still. This is going to sting."

Ryan had to admit to himself that he was impressed with how Lionel was taking care of him and watching out for him, even if Lionel put him down and called him names sometimes. This was clearly a kid who either had it in his personality or character to help others, or he had really paid attention when his parents took care of him.

Lionel pulled several squares of gauze off a roll, drenched them in a solution that smelled like a doctor's office, and told Ryan, "Close your eyes, grit your teeth, and stand still. It'll sting, but I have to clean that wound, and it won't hurt long. The air will cool it, and the pain will go away quick."

"Wait! Don't! Let me do it!"

"Yeah, sure. No way. Now come on and let me. Hurry, this stuff evaporates faster than water. Now do what I say."

Ryan held his breath and shut his eyes. He forgot to grit his teeth, but that happened automatically when Lionel set down the first-aid kit and gently touched the alcohol-drenched gauze to his raw, scraped forehead. Lionel didn't even rub it but it felt like sandpaper on Ryan's wound. Ryan started to wrench away from the pain, but Lionel seemed prepared for that. He grabbed Ryan's arm with his free hand and hung on. Ryan wanted to squeal, but he resisted, his teeth pressed tightly together.

"OK," Lionel said. "Hang on. I'm through and I'm going to let go. Just don't touch that spot. It's clean, and when it dries we can bandage it."

"Ooooh! Ooooh!" was all Ryan could say.

It felt as if it would sting forever, and it took all he had in him to keep from pressing his hand over it. But, just as Lionel had promised, in a few minutes the stinging began to fade. Soon it felt cool, then cold, then numb. "I think it's dry, Lionel," Ryan managed.

"Hold still again," Lionel said, tearing a huge bandage out of its wrapper.

"Be careful," Ryan warned.

"You sayin' I wasn't careful cleaning it?"

"No, just that—"

"This'll be the easy part. Now be brave."

Lionel was right. There was nothing to applying the bandage. Lionel kept the sticky stuff on the outside of the sore and pressed it tight. But Ryan didn't feel brave. He was feeling more and more like a little kid, and that made him mad. The trouble was, he couldn't be mad at Lionel, who was trying to toughen him up. He didn't want to be mad at his parents, though he couldn't shake the feeling that they should not have left him. He knew they hadn't meant to or chosen to, but that didn't make him feel any better. It was hard to be mad at God when you didn't believe in God. So that left only himself to be mad at for being such a weakling.

He didn't like that much. Having been a good athlete for as long as he could remember, he had never been scared of bullies or shy of older kids, unless they were way older and a lot bigger. Lionel would not have bothered him a week ago. But Ryan felt so alone, so lost. He hated the feeling and wished it would go away. But he missed his mom and dad so much he couldn't imagine that he would ever feel any better. This was no way to live, but he had to.

Ryan was grateful for Lionel's help. It was almost like having a parent for those few moments. But he wanted to know why Lionel was so serious and seemed so bothered, and he wanted to know now. "Why would I not want to go in the house?" he said.

"I don't know. Do you? Let's be brave. Let's go in. You'll be glad you did."

"Not until you tell me why you don't think I'll ever want to go in."

"All right," Lionel said. "Someone's been in there."

"What?! How do you—"

"Don't get so excited. What did you expect with all the police busy with everything else? Bad guys take advantage of these kinds of situations all the time."

"There's never been a time like this before, Lionel."

"I know, but in my uncle's neighborhood, anytime something big is happening in the city or there's a fire or anything, people get their houses robbed or looted. You just have to watch and be careful, that's all. The robbers aren't out to hurt anybody. They're just trying to get something for nothing. You have to make it hard for them to get in or easy for them to get out, and if you happen upon them, be sure they're scared enough to run off before you try to hassle them. Just like cornered animals, if they feel trapped, they'll attack. You don't want that."

"How do you know someone was in my house?"

"Because the glass in the back door was broken, the door was open, and lots of stuff is missing."

"Oh, no! Stuff we're going to need if we're going to stay alive?"

"No. All the food and everything is still there. These guys must have known what they wanted and what was valuable. Your TVs are gone, your stereo; looks like some jewelry is gone from your mother's dresser. That kind of stuff."

Ryan shook his head and sat in the driveway. "You're right," he said. "I don't ever want to go in there again."

"Don't you see, Ryan? If we lived in there, robbers would be afraid to take the risk. They'd see the lights and they'd figure adults

have to be in there. You never had anyone
break in before, did you?"

"Never."

"There you go. This was a normal house-
hold, people coming and going. It was too
risky to break into. Somebody just checked it
out while we were gone and thought maybe
the family had disappeared or were gone
somewhere during the emergency. They got
everything valuable there was to get, and they
won't need to come back."

"But what about someone else?"

"You never know."

"Then I'm not going in."

"Can I?"

"You want to live in my house?"

"Where else am I gonna live?"

"In your own house."

"Where've you been, Ryan? My house has
been taken over by my uncle's enemies, and
until the police have time to mess with getting
them out, I'm on the street. Now are you going
to let me stay in your house awhile, or not?"

"You really want to, knowing someone's
been in there? Aren't you scared?"

"I've got plenty to be scared about, Ryan,
just like you. But if anything happens to me,
I go to heaven to see my family. I'm not
sayin' I want to die, but I've got a lot more to
be afraid of than that some burglar is going

to come back to a house he already cleaned out."

"You're going to make me stay by myself in the tent?"

"That's up to you."

"I want to be where you are, and I want that to be outside with me."

"Ryan, I can't stand sleeping on the ground or even in a sleeping bag. I'll be miserable. You've got nice beds in the house, food, drinks, bathrooms. Come on, man, get a clue."

"I can't help it if I'm scared. It's not like I'm being this way on purpose. How about we just sit in the tent now and keep an eye on the house. Then when it gets dark and we get tired, maybe I'll want to sleep in a real bed."

"That'll be the day."

"Well, I'm not promising, but if you can fix that broken window, I'd feel a lot better."

There was nothing to boarding up a broken window either, Lionel told Ryan. "You got some plywood and a hammer and nails?"

"Sure."

"Let me at 'em."

Ryan was amazed again at what Lionel could do. "Your dad teach you all this stuff?"

"Yeah, I guess. I never thought about it as him teaching me. He just let me do stuff with him and would tell me what to do. It's not hard. It's just logical. You want to nail this board all the way around the window in the door so it keeps air and water out. It'll let you lock the door and keep you safe until you can get someone out here who knows how to install windows."

"I figured you could do that too."

Lionel shook his head and smiled a tight-lipped grin. "Nah. Dad and I just took care of the basics. Nothing fancy."

By the time the door was finished and the boys had sat in the tent a few hours, talking and watching the house, it began to grow dark. "You thinking what I'm thinking?" Lionel said.

"What, that you'd like to go in the house?"

"Uh-huh."

"No, actually I was thinking that I hoped you would stay in the tent one more night."

Lionel looked exhausted as he shook his head sadly. "You stay in this tent tonight, man, and you'll be here alone. I mean, it's not my place to invite myself into your house, but you've got to let me stay there, Ryan. OK?"

"I don't know."

"Sure you do, now come on! The longer you put off doing something you're afraid of, the harder it is to ever do it."

"I know."

"Then let's go."

"My head's kind of still hurting, and I've got a bruise in my side."

"From what?"

"When I fell. I hit something on the bike."

"Let me see that," Lionel said. He turned on a flashlight and Ryan lifted his shirt. "Ouch," Lionel said. "That must hurt."

"Does it need a bandage?"

"No, just looks like a deep bruise. It'll hurt for a while, but it'll go away. Your forehead or your side are no reason to not go into the house. In fact, you'll probably get better faster if you do go in."

"Could we do something first?"

"Like what?"

"Ride around, go somewhere. I'm bored."

"You're stalling."

"Yeah, but if we do that I'll get more tired and maybe then I'll want to go inside."

"All right, but like I told you, Ryan, if you don't go in the house tonight, you're going to be out here by yourself. I would think that would be scarier than being in your house with me."

Ryan believed that. He shrugged. "Maybe."

"So where do you want to go?"

"Maybe down to my friend Raymie's."

"You said he disappeared."

"Yeah, but I know his dad is home. And I

want to know if his sister is all right. She's off at college in California, and she's cool. Raymie actually liked his big sister. I'd never heard of that before."

"Hey, I liked my big sister too. It's not so unusual, especially if they're enough older than you. So, what, you want to go talk to Raymie's dad?"

"That'd be OK. Maybe he'd let us stay with him."

"*That* would make you feel safe, wouldn't it?"

"Yeah. Maybe he misses Raymie so much he'd like to have a boy his age around."

"You *want* an adult in charge of you? Freedom is the only part of this I'm already getting used to."

"Just let's go, OK?"

"OK, but I'm not for talking to the guy. How far is it?"

"Just down the block."

NINE

Together Again

It was well past dark, and Vicki had been sleeping on her back for more than nine hours, her feet flat on the floor at the end of the bed. Her eyes popped open, and she stared at the ceiling, wondering where she was. It came to her quickly.

Her mouth felt thick and dry, her eyes still heavy, and yet she felt rested. A deep emptiness borne of loss and sorrow overtook her, yet she was comforted as well by her new faith.

From the living room came the sound of the television. Judd must be up. She tiptoed out, only to find him curled up on the couch, still sleeping. So, she thought, neither of them had slept where they planned. She gently pulled the remote control from his hands and turned off the TV. Judd did not stir. She would take advantage of the time to get cleaned up and changed.

The hot shower felt so good she could hardly pull herself away from it. She didn't know if hot water was limited in a big house like this the way it was in a trailer where family members had to schedule their showers carefully. She hoped she'd saved enough hot water for Judd.

Vicki put on one of Mrs. Thompson's silky robes and sat drying her hair, then brushing it. She felt so much better than she had, and she had to admit she looked better too. It was time for a new look. All her own clothes had been lost in the fire, and that was for the best. While she didn't care to look like a mother of teenagers, as Mrs. Thompson was, neither did she ever want to go back to her old look.

Vicki was grateful to find that her feet were roughly the same size as Mrs. Thompson's had been. She hung up the pantsuit that had served as her blanket when she fell asleep. And she found a sweater, jeans, white socks, and tennis shoes. Vicki had no idea whether she and Judd would be going anywhere that evening, but these were good hanging-around-the-house clothes too. She had not dressed this way since she was a little girl. Not so many hours ago she would have considered this her least likely choice for an outfit. Yet as she looked in the mirror now, she felt it was a good look for her.

Vicki knew she and Judd might both regret having caught up on their sleep during the day. No way would they be tired at a normal bedtime. But he had said something earlier about trying to hook up with Bruce Barnes again that evening.

She would like that. Bruce was an interesting guy. He seemed to care about them so much, and yet he hardly knew them. She wanted to see his reaction when he found out that not just one, but both of them had become believers. And what about those two younger kids, Lionel and Ryan? Lionel had already become a Christian, but the other one, the little blond kid, had run off angry. Vicki couldn't blame him. How would she have felt in his situation, losing both parents and knowing they probably weren't in heaven?

Vicki hoped Lionel had found Ryan and had had some influence on him. She had been acquainted with Judd and Lionel and Ryan for such a short time, and yet she found herself already caring about what would become of them. These were all new emotions and feelings for her.

Vicki was hungry again. She moved into the living room to see if Judd was still asleep. He was gone, and she heard water running upstairs. If his shower felt as good as hers, he would feel a lot better. She rummaged in the kitchen for a snack for the two of them, set it up in front of the TV, and sat watching the news while waiting for him.

Lionel and Ryan had to stay on the other side of the street from the Steeles because a car was coming the other way and Lionel didn't want to risk crossing in front of it. He knew if he didn't, Ryan wouldn't. Lionel didn't understand why Ryan seemed so much younger when the difference in their ages was barely a year. But, if it was worth comparing their predicaments, he had to admit that Ryan was worse off than he was.

The headlights coming the other way did not pass the boys, however. They stopped in front of the Steele home, and Lionel noticed that the car was a cab.

"That's Raymie's sister, Chloe," Ryan said as a young woman emerged from the backseat. The cabby jumped out and pulled her huge suitcase from the trunk. He set it next to her as she dug in her purse for the fare. She was paying him when the front door of the house burst open and a tall dark man ran out in his stocking feet. As the cabby pulled away, Rayford Steele gathered his daughter into his arms.

"Oh, Daddy!" she wailed. "How's everybody?"

He backed away from her enough that she could see him shaking his head sadly.

"I don't want to hear this," she said, pulling away from him and looking to the house as if expecting to see her mother or brother.

"It's just you and me, Chloe," Mr. Steele said, and they stood together in the darkness, crying.

Lionel sensed Ryan getting ready to cross the street and greet them. "Not now," Lionel whispered. "There'll be plenty of time to talk to them. But not now."

As father and daughter made their way inside, Ryan said, "But I'm not ready to go back home yet."

"You wanna go to the church?" Lionel asked.

"What for?"

"To see if Bruce Barnes is still there."

"Why would I want to do that? I don't believe all that stuff he's saying, and even if it *is* true, it was mean of God to do that to us kids."

"We had our chances," Lionel said.

"*I* didn't."

"You said Raymie Steele told you about this a while ago."

"Yeah, well—"

"Yeah, well, I want to go see Bruce. You can wait here, go home alone, or whatever you want."

"I'll go, but I'm not coming in."

"Whatever."

Vicki felt a strange reaction when Judd came downstairs, cleaned up and dressed. He had shaved off his goatee, and he looked much younger. She still had no idea what she thought of him as a person. She was glad they might become friends, because she needed one and he seemed to know a lot about God and the Bible because of how he had been raised. Vicki had no feelings for him or romantic interest in him. It was way too early for that, and because of what she had been through, she wasn't even thinking that way.

But Judd seemed so impressed with her new look that she wondered if he was allowing himself to become interested in her. She talked herself out of it, however. It was impossible. He had been through as great a trauma as she had, and he had to be suffering privately as much as she. Anyway, he had seen where she lived. No way a guy like him would be interested in her.

"Oh, good," he said. "Food. What's on TV?"

"Same as what's been on the whole time since the disappearances. News, news, and more news."

Judd asked if she had seen the strange videotapes he had seen on the news earlier. So far she hadn't. "All they're talking about now," she said, "is this guy with a funny name from some country in eastern Europe. He became president of his country recently and—"

"And now he's coming to speak at the UN, right? Yeah, I heard about him. Nicholas something. And his last name sounds like a mountain range."

"Nicolae, I think," Vicki said. She hadn't picked up the last name either, but just then the young leader's picture came on the news again. She turned it up. The announcer referred to him as Nicolae Carpathia, the new president of Romania.

"You're right," Judd said. "Nicolae. And he must have been named after the Carpathian Mountains."

"Hey," Vicki said, "I thought you said you didn't do well in school. How do you know about those mountains?"

Judd looked embarrassed. "That's about all I know," he said. "Really, you just reached the end of my information."

They ate and watched the news for several minutes. Finally Vicki asked if he was still thinking about trying to see Bruce that night.

"Yeah, I was," he said. "You want to?"

"Sure."

"I'll call and make sure he's there."

Lionel and Ryan dragged their bikes inside the church and found Judd's bike there too. They poked around looking for Bruce, Lionel wondering if Judd was there or if he had just never taken his bike home. Lionel and Ryan found Bruce finishing up a session with several older people, but before he could greet them, Ryan said, "I'll be waiting by the bikes. I've heard all this before."

"C'mon, Ryan!"

"No!"

Lionel looked apologetically at Bruce when he approached. "Good to see you again, Lionel. Let me introduce you to these folks." Lionel couldn't keep track of the names except for one, Bruce's secretary, Loretta. She was old, had a southern accent, and seemed classy. Lionel knew if he was going to spend much time at this church, he ought to get to know her. Bruce whispered, "Ask her sometime to tell you her own story. It'll amaze you."

Lionel had been wondering how this handful of old people had been left behind. He figured anybody who had been around that long, especially churchgoers, would have learned the truth long ago. But then he had had time too and knew the truth. Like him, maybe, they simply didn't respond to it.

"Well, I found Ryan, as you can see."

"Yeah. Don't worry about him hanging back for a while. I'm sure he's embarrassed about bolting on us. If we don't scare him off, he'll come around and get curious and eventually join us again."

Lionel's look of doubt must have betrayed him.

"You don't agree?" Bruce said.

"I've been working on him," Lionel said. "And I know how important you say it is for him not to put this off."

"It is."

"But it's not like he's putting it off. It's more like he really doesn't understand or doesn't want to. Sometimes I think he understands fine but just doesn't believe in God."

Bruce shook his head and pulled up a

chair for Lionel. Bruce sat on the corner of a table, took off his wire-rimmed glasses, and ran his hand through his curly hair. "He'll believe in God before long, if there's any truth to what I've been studying. Everybody is going to know God is in this when the seven-year tribulation begins. People are going to be dying right and left, and we'd better be prepared. I'm so glad you made your decision right away, like I did. I know you're sorry you missed out on the Rapture, but there was sure no sense in waiting once we knew what happened, right?"

Lionel nodded. "I saw Judd's bike out there. Did he come back?"

"No. He left that here. But I did just get a call from him. He and Vicki are coming by this evening. He sounded a little more upbeat. I didn't talk to her, but I'm sure worried about them. Both of them are where you and I were, and I don't want them to keep finding reasons to put off coming to Christ."

Lionel told Bruce about his and Ryan's day. He was impressed that Bruce, as tired as he had to be, seemed interested in every detail. Bruce offered to drive Lionel back to the morgue in Chicago so he could identify his uncle's body. He said he would call the police about the intruders in his house and ask them to check Ryan's house too.

"I don't want you to have to worry about all that stuff," Lionel said. "Everybody you know is going to have a lot of this kind of stuff going on, and you can't do this for them all."

"So, you caught me in a generous mood. Take advantage of it. I need to stay busy. For one thing, I'm making up for lost time. But you must know I've got reasons to not want to go home too."

Lionel nodded. Who was supposed to take care of Bruce when Bruce was taking care of everybody else? Bruce told him there were several small groups he was meeting with. "I can tell adults a little more of what I'm going through, and they're supporting me as much as I'm supporting them. We're getting more and more calls every day from people who have had some contact with this church in the past. I think we're going to have quite a crowd here Sunday. People are desperate for answers. And we have them."

Lionel sat wishing Ryan would come in from the foyer. He kept looking back that way. "Was there something specific you wanted, Lionel?" Bruce asked.

"Me? No. I just wanted to check in with you. I've been wondering about those other two, too, and I was hoping we could work on them and Ryan."

"Ryan's going to be the toughest," Bruce said. "This is newer to him, and his parents are dead."

Ryan traded off sitting on the floor and moseying around the front of the church, idly looking at literature in the foyer. He was bored, but he had no interest in meeting with Bruce again. He had just pulled a tract off a table and began reading it, not understanding a bit of it, when Judd and Vicki came in. He looked at them and then looked away, embarrassed. He hoped they wouldn't say anything about his crying and running out.

"Hey, Ryan!" Vicki said. "Glad you came back. Where's Bruce?"

Ryan shrugged. "Somewhere with Lionel."

"Is it private or can we join them?"

Ryan shrugged again, wishing she would stop asking him questions. He didn't know and he didn't care.

"Hey," Judd said, "where are you guys staying?"

Now *there* was a question Ryan wanted to answer. He gushed the whole story about being scared to go in his own house and how

Lionel's place had been taken over by guys who might have murdered Lionel's uncle. He told them someone had broken into his house, just before he had almost talked himself into agreeing with Lionel that they *should* stay there.

"I've got plenty of room at my house," Judd said. "In fact—"

"You *do?*" Ryan said quickly. "That would be great. Can I stay with you even if Lionel doesn't want to?"

"Slow down there, little man," Judd said. "We can all talk about this together and see what Bruce thinks about it. Vicki and I have some news for all of you anyway. Come on, let's find Lionel and Bruce."

"I don't want to."

"Why not?"

"Same reason as the other night. I don't believe this stuff."

"Well, you probably will."

"No, I won't."

"Even if you don't, we're all in this thing together. We have to watch out for each other. We need each other."

"You just want to talk me into this."

"Nobody can do that, little man. It means nothing anyway unless you decide on your own."

"I want to stay out here."

Ryan was worried that he had disappointed Judd, who looked peeved.

"What if I said you could only stay with me if you come in and see Bruce?"

"I guess I'd have to then," Ryan muttered. "You're probably going to force me to become a Christian too."

"No, I won't do that. Nobody can do that."

"What about you guys? Are you Christians now too, like Lionel?"

Judd appeared to be about to answer when Vicki interrupted. "He can find out at our meeting with Bruce, Judd. I mean, if he'd really rather stay here, he can just wait to see what we talked about."

"Good idea," Judd said. "What's it going to be, Ryan?"

"Do you promise to quit calling me 'little man'?"

"Sure. Now quit stalling."

"I want to stay here," he said.

"It's your call," Judd said, turning to head into the sanctuary.

"I hope you don't regret it," Vicki said, not in a mean way. In fact, Ryan thought she seemed so nice, he wouldn't have minded going in with them.

They were almost out of sight when he muttered, "Wait up. I'm coming."

TEN

The Mystery

JUDD was glad Ryan Daley had followed Vicki and him to find Bruce and Lionel. He had a feeling this was going to be a good meeting, regardless of what Ryan decided. Still, despite his anticipation of telling Bruce his and Vicki's good news, Judd couldn't shake the turmoil deep inside him. He wondered whether, even if he survived the seven years of tribulation that was to come, he would ever forget his regret, his remorse, and the bitter loss of his family.

He tried to push that aside for now, knowing that everyone who had been left behind faced the same anxiety. Bruce opened their little meeting with prayer. Then he asked each person to bring the group up to date since the last time they had been together.

Judd was first, and he told of his and Vicki's talks, of their adventure at O'Hare, and added that he would leave it for Vicki to tell about what she found at her home and what spiritual decision she had come to. "As for me," he said, "I finally realized I was being stubborn and stupid to put off doing something I should have done years ago."

When Bruce realized what Judd was saying, he immediately stood and leaned down to embrace him. Judd felt awkward and embarrassed. His dad had not been much for hugging, especially after Judd got to be about twelve, but still he was glad Bruce seemed so genuinely happy for him. Bruce was on the verge of tears when he said, "Lionel and I welcome you to the family. We're all brothers in Christ."

Lionel reached out a congratulatory fist, and Judd met it with his own. Then it was Vicki's turn. "I'm going to keep this short, Bruce, because you look like you could use some sleep—"

"Oh, don't worry about me."

"—And I'm going to tell it in the order it happened." Her story was much like Judd's, of course, and when she got to the part where she prayed to receive Christ, Bruce embraced her too and welcomed her as a sister in the family. Lionel reached out his fist and she patted it, making him chuckle. Judd was too embarrassed to hug her, so he shook her hand. Meanwhile, it appeared Ryan was just taking this all in.

When Vicki told of finding the burned out shell of her trailer, Bruce looked startled. He did not appear pleased to hear that she seemed to be planning to stay with Judd for a while. Judd felt he had to explain.

"We're not going together or even interested in anything like that," he said. "And we would stay on different floors. We're more like brother and sister, like you said."

"I'd feel more comfortable if I could find you a woman from the church to stay with, like my secretary. She has a big home with lots of room. And she's by herself now."

"I don't think I want to do that," Vicki said. "This doesn't have to look bad, and if it does, it's only because people are assuming the wrong thing."

Bruce looked as if he wanted to talk about it some more, but instead he urged Vicki to continue with her story.

"That's all, really."

Bruce called on Lionel, who gave a rundown on all that he and Ryan had been through. Judd was surprised that he seemed to speak for Ryan, but it was also likely that Ryan didn't want to talk anyway. If Lionel didn't tell Ryan's part, no one would. Judd was amazed at all they had been through in such a short time. Was this what it was going to be like, then? Nothing but trouble around the clock? And how awful about Lionel's uncle! "I can take you to that high school where the morgue is," Judd offered.

"I've already got that covered," Bruce said. "I'll call to see where they're shipping the bodies, because surely no high school has the equipment to hold bodies for long. We'll find out where Lionel's uncle André is, and we'll get him over there to identify the body."

Bruce asked Ryan if he wanted to say anything. That was when Judd noticed that Ryan still had the tract he had taken from the foyer. He was pretending to study it, but he'd had time to read it over and over if he wanted. Ryan said nothing. He just shook his head.

"Fair enough," Bruce said. "No one's going to pressure you. You can be a part of this group as long as you want, regardless of what you decide to do. When you're ready, you make this decision on your own."

Finally, Ryan spoke. "And what if my decision is to say no?"

Bruce said, "Nobody can make the decision for you. You have to live with the consequences."

"Or die with them," Lionel said.

Now Ryan was mad. Judd thought he might bolt again. "He's been talking to me that way all day," Ryan said. "What kind of a Christian is that?"

"I've only been kidding. Kids our age crack on people all the time. Can't you take it?"

"This has to be a fragile time for him," Bruce said.

"It's that way for all of us," Lionel said. "But that doesn't mean we have to be so touchy."

"I just want you to quit hassling me, Lionel. OK?"

Lionel shrugged. "I guess. If it's bothering you that much."

"It is."

"So if I start talking nicer to you, will you—"

Bruce held up a hand. "No deals, no bribes, no pressure, remember?"

Lionel nodded. "Sorry."

Judd wanted to make his offer. "I'd like both of you guys to stay at my place too."

"I was hoping you'd say that," Ryan said.

"I'd feel better about Vicki staying there if the other two were there too," Bruce said.

Judd felt some of his old rebellion surfacing. He resented Bruce's implying that Judd was responsible to him. Maybe Bruce considered himself Judd's pastor already, and because he was older he thought he could boss him around. Judd thought maybe he *did* need somebody doing that, but his first reaction came from the person he used to be. He didn't like being told what to do. What kind of a Christian was he going to be? Well, Bruce seemed more comfortable with everybody staying in the same house, so maybe it wouldn't be an issue again. Judd hoped not.

After the meeting the kids filed into Bruce's office, where he began calling around to find out who in Chicago would know anything about Lionel's uncle André. The phones still gave everyone fits, and between busy signals, bad connections, and the usual runarounds and red tape everyone had to go through, it appeared to Judd that Bruce was getting to the end of his rope.

Finally someone was able to tell him that the bodies that had been delivered to the high school in André's neighborhood would be available for identification at a city morgue in a nearby precinct late Friday afternoon, two days away.

"I'll take you then," Bruce told Lionel. Then he helped load Ryan's, Lionel's, and Judd's bikes into the trunk of Judd's car.

They took up so much room that Judd had to leave the trunk open as the four of them clambered in for the ride to his house.

Judd rolled down his window and called out to Bruce. "You sure you wouldn't rather stay with us too?"

"Only if you really need me," Bruce said. Judd was relieved. He wished Bruce had a place to stay that wouldn't be so painful for him. But the independent part of Judd also liked the idea that he would be the oldest in the house, and the house was his, after all. He didn't know if he was up to being in charge of three people he hardly knew, but he was eager to find out.

Being in charge was not at all what Judd expected. For the next few days it seemed all he did was worry what Vicki was thinking, referee arguments between Ryan and Lionel, and try to explain why he and Vicki got the "good" rooms and the other two got the leftovers. He had no say over when anybody came and went. He wasn't their parent or their boss, as they reminded him often. He suddenly realized how tough it would be to be a parent whose kid or kids didn't respect him or listen to him or obey him. He was getting a clear view of what a problem he had been to his parents.

Judd spent a lot of time digging through his dad's papers, finding out what bills had to be paid and when. He also found the documents that told him where his father had his money deposited and what accounts had balances. Judd was grateful to realize that his father was a good money manager and planner, and that there was more than enough there to last anyone ten years, let alone seven, if he was careful.

Judd gave Vicki cash to buy herself some clothes, and she proved to be very frugal. She told him that if she could really use his mother's stuff, she wouldn't need much more. And she kept insisting that she would get a job and pay him back. "You really don't need to," Judd said. "There's plenty more money."

"So I'm just supposed to become a bum and let someone else pay for everything for me? I don't think so, Judd. I mean, I appreciate it, but what kind of pride would I have if I let you do that?"

Judd didn't know what to say. Ryan said he would be happy to let Judd pay for everything, but Lionel shamed him into admitting that he would only feel good about himself too if he was earning some money to contribute to the pot.

Bruce phoned Judd's home during the middle of the afternoon that Friday. "Judd," he said, "I hate to do this to you, but I'm going to need you to bail me out. I've got people calling right and left and I'm meeting with them, counseling them, you name it. I've gotten nowhere in trying to prepare for Sunday, and it looks like we're going to be jam-packed."

"What do you need?" Judd asked.

"I need you to drive Lionel in to that morgue. It's not in a good part of town, and I know you have not dealt with Chicago authorities before, but if I tell you whom to ask for and what to say, can you handle it?"

"Sure."

"And you'll let me know as soon as you get back, so I'll know you're safe?"

Judd hesitated.

"Judd?"

"Well . . ."

"You don't want to do it? I understand. I'll get someone el—"

"No, it's not that. I just want to talk to you about checking in with you to let you know I'm safe and all that. I don't want to get into that trap."

"I'm only asking you this time because I'm

asking you to do something as a favor for
me—something I should be doing myself."

"Yeah, OK. I don't mind."

Bruce gave Judd all the information and
directions. Surprisingly, not only did Ryan
want to go along, but so did Vicki. Judd talked
them out of it. "It's not a good part of town,"
he said. "I figure there'll be lots of cops there,
and if they see a bunch of kids, they might
have a lot of questions. Just let Lionel and me
do this, and when we get back we'll tell you
all about it."

Vicki found it strange to be alone in the house
with Ryan. They had not talked much, and he
didn't seem interested in starting. She tried to
make small talk with him, but she didn't get
far. He had already heard her life story and
what had been happening to her lately. She
tried to interest him in the news, then remembered that he had been watching the news
when he learned of his father's death. She
wanted to comfort him, encourage him, point
him toward God, but she was at a loss. She
had no idea how to reach him.

"I promised Bruce we would all be in church
Sunday morning," she tried at one point.

"You didn't promise him for me, I hope," Ryan said. "Everybody's always deciding for me what I'm going to do."

"You don't want to go?"

"'Course not. Haven't you figured that out yet?"

"I know you don't believe this stuff yet, but I'd think you'd want to check it out. Aren't you curious what Bruce is going to say to all the people who come looking for answers? I think it'll be cool just to see how many show up, what they're thinking, and how Bruce does. He says he's never really been a preacher, but he can't wait to tell these people about Jesus."

Ryan clammed up then.

"Well, I *did* tell Bruce I thought we would all be there," Vicki added. "But *you* made no promises, so it's up to you."

"I'll probably come," Ryan said, as if he had no choice. Vicki thought that showed progress. It was totally up to him, and he was pretending to reluctantly go along.

Ryan wandered up to his room, the one that used to belong to Judd's little brother, Marc. Vicki got out the Bible Bruce had given her and started reading in the New Testament where he had told her to begin. Who would have ever thought, she wondered, that she would want to read the Bible at all, let alone on her own when no one was making her?

Lionel wasn't comfortable with Judd yet. As they rode into Chicago, he found himself having to work at holding his end of the conversation. He was sort of amused at Judd. He had been a rich kid from a good home who had tried to blend in with the bad kids and the rebels. Lionel knew the type. He found Judd sort of plain and not at all a tough guy or streetwise. That made it funny to him that Judd had tried to be something he was not. In fact, he was so far from the image he had tried to project that it was laughable.

Lionel had to admit that Judd had changed pretty quickly. With the goatee gone and him no longer wearing all black, Judd started to look like a normal, suburban teen.

Lionel asked him about the details of the visit to the morgue. When Judd told him what Bruce had spelled out, Lionel said, "You know, I think I can handle this myself. Your car is not going to be safe down there, so you should probably stay with it. I won't be long."

Lionel thought Judd would put up a fuss,

insisting on talking with the authorities himself. So far Judd had seemed to enjoy playing the big shot. But to Lionel's surprise, Judd seemed relieved. "Yeah, OK," he said quickly. "That's probably a good idea. I'll stay with the car, you do this stuff, and then we'll be out of there."

When Judd finally pulled in to the small, fenced lot behind the gray morgue building, he handed Lionel the sheet with the contact name. "I'll be right out," Lionel said.

He had prepared himself, he thought, for this moment. He had to be sure André was dead, and there was no better way than to see his body for himself. Lionel had always hated funerals, and he had been to his share for someone thirteen years old. What he hated most was the filing past the bodies. He always peeked at them, but he didn't stop and linger. He knew this would not be easy.

He had seen a lot of movies where someone had to identify a body. The coroner or medical examiner or whoever would dramatically yank the sheet away, and the identifier would collapse from the shock. Lionel didn't want that to happen. He knew André was in danger most of his life, and whether he really killed himself or had been murdered, it was no surprise that he had come to the end so soon. But he didn't want to be shocked by some horrible sight.

Lionel had stepped from the car with confidence, telling himself to just do his duty and get it over with. It made him feel grown up to handle this for his parents. He wished he could see them and his brother and sisters, but he was sure glad they weren't dead.

And yet as Lionel neared the front of the building, it was as if his legs had turned to jelly. He began to shudder and tremble, and he found it difficult to put one foot in front of the other. His breath came in short gasps, and he fought the urge to race back to the car and have Judd run him back to Mount Prospect. *I'm going to do this*, he thought. *I have to. Otherwise, I'll be a wuss, just like Ryan.*

Lionel put his hand on the brass handle of the front door and stopped. It was as if he was paralyzed, his legs heavy. The handle felt icy, though it was not that cold out. He forced himself to pull the heavy door open, and he was immediately struck with fear and dread by what he saw. This was nothing at all like he had assumed. The entire place had been turned into a storage area for white-sheeted bodies.

Lionel thought a morgue had one area for bodies in drawers. He knew that was true, but it shouldn't have surprised him to find this morgue overcrowded, what with everything that had gone on.

Lionel felt the cold rush from the air conditioners. This place, the whole building, was cold as a refrigerator. Covered bodies were lined up on stretchers down both sides of the hallway, and Lionel could only assume that's the way it was all through the building.

A bored receptionist in a winter coat said, "You can't be in here, son. What are you doing?"

"I'm here to identify a body," he said.

"All the bodies in here have been identified," she said.

Lionel dug the sheet of instructions from his pocket. "I'm looking for assistant medical examiner Ford," he said.

The receptionist paged him. "You'd better take a seat," she said. "No telling how long he'll be."

He was twenty minutes, time enough for Lionel to calm himself if he was able. But he was not able. All the wait did was to make him more upset. He wanted to be anywhere other than this creepy place. None of the dead bodies he had ever seen before were related to him. He had no idea how he would react.

Dr. Ford was a pudgy man in a hurry, and

he was all business. "You're Washington? Where's Barnes?"

"Couldn't make it," Lionel said.

"This way, Washington."

Lionel followed the fast-walking doctor down the halls between the stretchers with bodies on them. He held his breath and looked neither right nor left. The doctor peeled a couple of sheets of paper back off his clipboard and studied a page. "André Dupree, right?"

"Yes, sir."

"Age 36, male, African-American, 5 foot 8, 155 pounds?"

"That's him."

"He's in the back. You OK?"

"Yeah, just a little out of breath."

"Almost there."

"Could you do it slow?"

"What, walking? Lots to do, son. Never seen this many deaths in so short a time. Never anything like it."

"No, I mean, will you show me his body slow?"

"Meaning?"

"Like, don't whip the sheet off."

"I never do that."

"Good."

When Dr. Ford got to the back, the place looked more like what Lionel expected. Six bodies were lined up next to each other. The doctor lifted the bottom of the sheets and read the tags on the toes of two in the middle. "Dupree," he said. "Here are his effects, if you want them. We threw away the jeans. They were, um, stained with blood."

"Lots of it?"

"'Fraid so. This was a suicide, you know."

"I figured." Lionel was having trouble speaking loudly enough to be heard. He still wasn't sure he could keep from running out of there. The doctor handed him a manila envelope clasped by a red string. He unwound it with shaky fingers and saw his uncle's watch, bracelet, earring, ring, beeper, belt, and socks.

"He came in here with that and a pair of jeans and stocking feet."

Lionel nodded, dreading what was to come.

The doctor moved to the other end of the stretcher. "Ever done this before, son?"

Lionel shook his head.

"I'm just going to fold the sheet back to his chest and you can see his face."

"And then I identify him to you?"

"That's not necessary. Identity is not in question in this case. The personal effects were on the body and in the pockets. A neighbor identified him. He was in his own apartment. You can just look away for a moment if you'd like."

Lionel held the envelope in both hands, as if he were holding a hat in front of him. He heard the slow rustle of the sheet. "OK, son," Dr. Ford said.

Lionel stared, speechless, at the expressionless face, and his heart seemed to stop. He could hear himself breathing. He wanted to say something, but words would not come.

"All right?" the doctor said.

Lionel nodded, his lips quivering.

"Can you find your way out?" Dr. Ford said.

Lionel nodded again and hurried toward the door. He was afraid he was going to be sick. The corridors looked longer than ever, and he couldn't wait to get out to the warmth of the day. By the time he reached the receptionist's area he was running. He burst through the door and sprinted to the parking lot, jumping into the car.

"You look like you saw a ghost," Judd said, starting the car.

Lionel could only snort.

"Oh, sorry, man," Judd said. "I guess you sorta did, huh?"

Lionel nodded.

"That his stuff there?"

"Uh-huh." It was the first sound Lionel had emitted since seeing the body.

"Did he look like himself?" Judd asked.

"I wouldn't know," Lionel said. "He probably did. The only thing I know for sure is that that was *not* my uncle."

ABOUT THE AUTHORS

Jerry B. Jenkins (www.jerryjenkins.com) is the writer of the Left Behind series. He is author of more than one hundred books, of which eleven have reached the *New York Times* best-seller list. Former vice president for publishing for the Moody Bible Institute of Chicago, he also served many years as editor of *Moody* magazine and is now Moody's writer-at-large.

His writing has appeared in publications as varied as *Reader's Digest, Parade,* in-flight magazines, and many Christian periodicals. He has written books in four genres: biography, marriage and family, fiction for children, and fiction for adults.

Jenkins's biographies include books with Hank Aaron, Bill Gaither, Luis Palau, Walter Payton, Orel Hershiser, Nolan Ryan, Brett Butler, and Billy Graham, among many others.

Eight of his apocalyptic novels—*Left Behind, Tribulation Force, Nicolae, Soul Harvest, Apollyon, Assassins, The Indwelling,* and *The Mark*—have appeared on the Christian Booksellers Association's best-selling fiction list and the *Publishers Weekly* religion best-seller list. *Left Behind* was nominated for Book of the Year by the Evangelical Christian Publishers Association in 1997, 1998, 1999, and 2000. *The Indwelling* was number one on the *New York Times* best-seller list for four consecutive weeks.

As a marriage and family author and speaker, Jenkins has been a frequent guest on Dr. James Dobson's *Focus on the Family* radio program.

Jerry is also the writer of the nationally syndicated sports story comic strip *Gil Thorp,* distributed to newspapers across the United States by Tribune Media Services.

Jerry and his wife, Dianna, live in Colorado.

Dr. Tim LaHaye (www.timlahaye.com), who conceived the idea of fictionalizing an account of the Rapture and the Tribulation, is a noted author, minister, and nationally recognized speaker on Bible prophecy. He is the founder of both Tim LaHaye Ministries and The Pre-Trib Research Center. Presently Dr. LaHaye speaks at many of the major Bible prophecy conferences in the U.S. and Canada, where his nine current prophecy books are very popular.

Dr. LaHaye holds a doctor of ministry degree from Western Theological Seminary and the doctor of literature degree from Liberty University. For twenty-five years he pastored one of the nation's outstanding churches in San Diego, which grew to three locations. It was during that time that he founded two accredited Christian high schools, a Christian school system of ten schools, and Christian Heritage College.

Dr. LaHaye has written over forty books, with over 30 million copies in print in thirty-three languages. He has written books on a wide variety of subjects, such as family life, temperaments, and Bible prophecy. His current fiction works, written with Jerry Jenkins—*Left Behind, Tribulation Force, Nicolae, Soul Harvest, Apollyon, Assassins, The Indwelling,* and *The Mark*—have all reached number one on the Christian best-seller charts. Other works by Dr. LaHaye are *Spirit-Controlled Temperament; How to Be Happy Though Married; Revelation Unveiled; Understanding the Last Days; Rapture under Attack; Are We Living in the End Times?;* and the youth fiction series Left Behind: The Kids.

He is the father of four grown children and grandfather of nine. Snow skiing, waterskiing, motorcycling, golfing, vacationing with family, and jogging are among his leisure activities.

The Future Is Clear

Check out the exciting Left Behind: The Kids series

Books #19 and #20 coming soon!

Discover the latest about the Left Behind series and complete line of products at

www.leftbehind.com